DIRTY ROGUE

AMELIA WILDE

DIRTY ROGUE

I'm a billionaire. I have *everything*—good looks, high-society friends, all the money I could want.

That doesn't mean I'm not a monster.

Sure, I'll go to parties. I'll pretend that life is carefree, an endless vacation with breaks to go to the office.

I can't ever get close to anyone.

Enter Quinn Campbell.

She has a fiery personality that even a New York City thunderstorm can't quench. When I see her for the first time, she's soaked to the skin and so gorgeous I don't feel the rain.

I can't let it be the last time.

I have to have her.

Even if it means revealing my darkest secret...

PROLOGUE

Ten years ago

The needle of the tattoo machine bites into the skin of my brother's chest. I can hear its pulsing hum above the music echoing off the brightly painted walls of the shop. It's some kind of pop-metal that was popular a couple years ago and has since fallen off the mainstream radar. My brother grins up at me from where he's lying back in the chair, completely relaxed even though the entire process appears painful. "It's not that bad."

I roll my eyes. "It looks delightful."

The tattoo artist, a young man with a serious expression, skin covered in tattoos, pauses to wipe some blood from his skin.

"You good?" he asks my brother.

"Yeah. Keep going."

"Dad's going to be pissed," I say lamely. It's the same argument I've been making since this morning, when my twin brother started pestering me about the tattoos—again—as we drove together in the Town Car on the way to our hometown of Dalton. It's our eighteenth birthday.

"He won't, and you know it," my brother laughs.

He's right in one sense. Dad won't be upset with Chris, but he'll find a way to make me feel like an idiot, one way or another. It'll either be that I shouldn't have gotten such a dumbass tattoo, or that I should have gone along with my brother's idea. I can never tell with our dad. We don't *get* each other.

The design is coming together on his skin. As far as tattoos go, it's pretty awesome—it's a reproduction of the Pierce family crest, but with one small alteration. Instead of the falcon that appears in one tiny portion of the crest, there's a C. You'd never notice it unless you knew it was there.

The benefit to having an identical twin is that if he's the reckless one, you can stand back to see how things turn out before you jump in feet first.

And in my case, my brother *is* the reckless one.

Everyone worships him. That's probably why he's our dad's favorite. My dad was the king of his frat in college. He still loves to party, but now that he's one of the richest men in New York, he doesn't take it quite as far as he used to. Everyone loves him because he's so much *fun*. It's the same thing with Chris.

For such a "fun guy," Dad can be an asshole. As far as I know, not being the life of the party isn't a crime.

I shove my hands into the pockets of my jeans. Not being at

the top of my dad's popularity list probably has to do with Mom. I'm too much like her.

But I'm not the one who divorced him.

"Come on, Eli. It's going to be awesome. Everyone's going to love it."

I smile in spite of myself. "If I wait, we can test it out."

"Testing things out" is something you only get to do if you're exact replicas of one another, which is the case with my brother and me. The differences between us—at least physically—are so subtle, so tiny, that we've successfully tricked our parents on more than one occasion. Not many people are going to be looking for the pinprick of a mole that Chris has on his left ankle. We're talking *that* miniscule level of shit. In every other way, looking at him is like looking into a mirror.

Personality-wise, we're night and day.

I've always been hesitant; he's always been the go-getter. I'll go after the things I want, but in general, I'll think it over first. Chris never does.

"What would we need to test it on?" he says, arching an eyebrow.

"Girls."

Chris scoffs. "You think *girls* aren't going to like a tattoo? You're crazy, man." The tattoo artist cracks a smile, but he doesn't look up from his work.

"Well, *certain* girls."

That's another difference between Chris and me. His attention tends to....*wander*. Chris dates a new girl every week, and they're typically the kind who like to get right down to screwing in the backseat of someone's car or their parents' spare room.

I've dated a few girls, and it's always been a long-term kind of thing. At least, as long-term as it gets during high school. Date someone a year and you're practically married.

Which, it turns out, is too boring for some people—namely, my last girlfriend, Sarah. She liked that I could afford to take her on all the fancy dates she wanted. What she *didn't* like was that I wouldn't sneak out with her as often as she wanted.

Not that my Dad would know, or care.

Unless it's on a day when he decides that he does, and then there's hell to pay.

Whatever. I'd rather not go through the hassle of buying my way out of some underage drinking charge.

Or worse.

Christian has been going to parties most every weekend, and I know he's doing more than drinking at those things. I can see it by the hazy glaze in his eyes some mornings, even if he won't admit it to me.

Even my fun-loving father doesn't get behind drugs.

This weekend, Chris is throwing a party at one of my father's rentals in the city. It's a massive penthouse that's currently between renters. What's convenient is that Dad leaves tomorrow for a five-day business trip to survey some of Pierce Industries' factories in China, so there'll be plenty of time to have the place cleaned after the party.

It's not the state of the penthouse carpet that has me worried. When I asked Chris earlier this week what type of party he was planning to have, he looked away before he answered.

"Just drinks," he lied.

It won't be just drinks.

"What are you going to do, Eli? Are you too much of a *delicate flower* to go through with this?"

"No," I say, shooting him one of my "I can be as cool as you" looks. The tattoo artist makes a few more strokes on the design, and then it's finished.

Chris is right. It looks cool as hell.

And maybe it's lame, but I want to impress him.

"I'm doing it," I say confidently.

Chris reaches out with his free arm and gives me a fist bump. "I knew you would."

"It looks sick," I say, as the tattoo artist wipes down Chris's arm with rubbing alcohol and begins applying Vaseline to keep the new pièce de résistance moist.

"Yeah, it does," Chris says, bending his neck down to get his first real look at it. "Think, Eli. You'll finally be edgy. How will the ladies resist?"

1

QUINN

I've been in New York City for five minutes, and it's already spitting on me.

Literally.

The moment I step out from the terminal into the taxi line, the heavy gray clouds that have been hanging ominously low over the city open up. The roof over the taxi stand isn't worth a damn against the rain, which is being driven by a squally summer wind, and of course I'm not wearing a raincoat and I don't have an umbrella.

The last thing I'm going to do is drag my oversized suitcase, stuffed with the clothes and books I couldn't bear to leave behind in Colorado, onto a city bus.

All I want to do is get to my new apartment, but the city is not playing fair.

What a welcome.

I square my shoulders. The one positive in this situation is that my traveling outfit consists of a black tank top and yoga pants, far better than the thin, pale pink t-shirt a woman three places ahead of me in line is wearing. She doesn't have a raincoat, either.

The line inches forward, and finally it's my turn to get into one of the waiting taxis.

I yank on the handle of the back door to the cab, only to discover that–of course–it sticks, and I narrowly avoid falling backward into the man waiting behind me in line. With another jerk on the door handle, it finally releases and the door opens on squeaky hinges.

This has to be the most run-down cab in the entire city. A fine layer of grime seems to cover every available surface of the vehicle and it reeks of stale cigarettes. Country music blares from the front of the cab.

No problem, I reassure myself in my most upbeat mental voice. *It's only going to be half an hour.*

I slide along the torn and patched back seat and wrestle my suitcase in beside me—there's no way I'm going to deal with the trunk—and then I lean awkwardly over it to haul the door closed. The taxi driver leers at me in the rearview mirror.

Gritting my teeth, I give him a smile, my lips pressed together tightly.

"Where to, sweetheart?" he rasps, not turning to face me.

I had memorized the address of my new place—well, my friend Carolyn's place—and I rattle it off to him, doing my best to sound as if it's not my first time in New York City.

"*Great*," says the driver in his raspy voice, as he steers the taxi away from the curb. "That'll give us *plenty* of time to get to know one another."

His voice makes my skin crawl, but I've been traveling all day. I'm only half an hour away from my new apartment. I'd give this creep a piece of my mind, but I don't have it in me right now. Instead, I pull out my phone to scan through my social media accounts.

That doesn't last long. It was terrible enough to find out that my fiancé, Derek, had been cheating on me for a year with my best friend. *Former* best friend. On top of that, now every time I open one of my social media apps, there's another message from a well-meaning friend or rabid gossip hawk wanting to know *what happened?!?!? You two always seemed so happy together.*

I swallow the lump in my throat and open the Maps app, watching the small blue dot representing the cab hurtle down the expressway at fifteen over.

The driver swerves the taxi into the opposite lane. The jolt throws me into the door next to me, and seconds later the red Ford Explorer he cut off speeds up alongside us, the driver red in the face and shaking his fist at us. My heart pounds. What is *wrong* with this guy?

Now that we're on I-495, there's nowhere for me to get out.

The cabbie raises his middle finger at the driver of the Explorer and bursts forth a croaky guttural laugh. Then he glances back into the mirror to look at me.

"Enjoying the ride?"

"No," I say flatly. I don't necessarily want to antagonize this asshole, but with this kind of ride, there will be no tip. "Please slow down."

The driver taps the brakes abruptly, then lets out another cackle. "Sure thing, sweetie. I'll slow down, and we can talk."

"I'm not in the mood to talk," I say, reaching over to my suitcase and tightening my grip on the handle. The second—and I mean the very *instant*—we're in Manhattan, I'm bailing.

Cars screech their brakes around us and drivers honk their horns furiously at our cab, which is crawling along at something like twenty miles per hour.

I'm about to open my mouth and demand that he drive like a normal person, when he speeds up again.

Yep. I'm in a cab driven by an insane person. Seriously, he must be crazy. I could die trying to get to my new apartment. Wouldn't *that* be rich?

It's like New York City doesn't want me here.

"Where you from, doll?" he comments like nothing has happened, and my stomach turns over.

My cell phone rings. My realtor's name flashes on the screen, and I'm seized by a wild hope. Maybe she found a buyer for my house already.

"Hello?" I answer, shouting over the loud country music still blaring from the cab's radio.

"Ms. Campbell?" my realtor says. She's a woman who always looks a little frazzled and right now she sounds that way, too. "Can you hear me?"

"I can hear you." I hunch down in the seat and cup my hand over my mouth. "What's going on?"

"Well—" she says, and I can practically hear her psyching up to give me bad news. "There's been a problem with your plumbing."

"The *plumbing*?" This is a new one. When I left my house, it was in perfect condition, ready to be sold. As quickly as possible.

"Yes. Unfortunately, some pipes have burst in the basement level, and there's no way we can proceed with showings unless..."

I tip my head back against the filthy seat and close my eyes, letting her voice fade into the background. New York City doesn't want me, and Colorado won't pull its claws out of my flesh.

"Thanks, Sherrie," I say when her voice finally peters out. "I'll get in touch with someone local to make the repairs right away." *As soon as I've survived this death trap of a cab ride.*

The driver makes a sharp turn, cutting across another lane of traffic. I end the call.

"So," he calls back over the music, licking his lips, "you need help with some plumbing? I'm available right now, hot stuff."

He winks. *Winks.*

Gross. I'm done.

"Stop the cab," I yell over the music, my voice cold and angry.

He bursts out laughing. "Sweetie, don't take it so personally. We're kidding around. We're having a good time."

"Stop the cab!" I shout, louder this time. "Right now, or I'm calling 9-1-1." I hold up my phone so he can see it in the rearview mirror, my finger poised on the button.

The leering smile leaves his face as his mouth twists into a scowl.

"Fine, bitch," he spits, then jerks on the wheel, cutting across a lane of traffic to reach the curb.

I'm out the door even as he begins to scream at me, incoherently, and the suitcase fights me too, sticking inside the door.

"Hey! Hey!" I finally make out some of the words. "You owe me! You *owe me*!"

"No way," I shout back at him, putting all my weight into getting my suitcase out of the car. I manage to wrench it free before the psycho pulls away, practically foaming at the mouth. And—crap. I never got his cab number or even looked at his information.

Now I'm standing in the rain, still several blocks away from my new apartment, and I have a massive suitcase to haul with me.

But I'm still alive.

Things could be worse.

A car zooms by too close to the curb, splashing me with another layer of dirty rainwater.

Could be worse.

2

CHRISTIAN

It's Pierce Industries' biggest event of the year, and I've got women on my mind.

Two, specifically. One, Angela, has been sending me text messages all evening. Photos with hot little captions. In each photo, she's wearing one less piece of clothing, and it's only 7:30. By the time I get out of here she should be wearing absolutely nothing. I sneak looks at my phone every few minutes as I continue pretending to appreciate the live jazz band playing tunes from a small raised stage at the far end of the ballroom.

Unfortunately for Angela—and despite how tempting the smooth curves of her body look in the photos—she's no longer an option. We've been on three dates, the absolute maximum number of dates I ever go on with a woman.

I can't let her get any closer.

The thought creeps into my mind like a foggy paranoia, and I brush it away. A tuxedoed waiter whisks past balancing a full tray of champagne flutes, the bubbly liquid glittering inside, and I grab one. It's the next best thing to sneaking out the back entrance and heading straight to the Purple Swan or my penthouse.

I'm lifting it to my lips when the second woman who has dibs on my attention slinks up next to me in a silky red dress that leaves little to the imagination. "*Another* drink?" she teases, her smile amped up with dark red lipstick. It's a little too much for my taste, but Christian Pierce isn't particular about shit like makeup.

I give her a sly half smile. "Melody. We keep running into each other."

"It's a small ballroom." She swipes a glass of champagne off another waiter's tray for herself, giving him a saucy wink as he goes by. "You're quite the attraction tonight, Mr. Pierce," she says, glancing sideways at me. Her lips don't leave a stain on the edge of the glass. How the hell do lipstick manufacturers pull *that* off?

As if to prove her point, three high-ranking partners, all about my father's age, approach me right then, their voices loud and boisterous. They've clearly been taking a little heavier advantage of the open bar than I have.

One of them, Stuart, shakes my hand, then claps me on the back. "You've finally made it, son. Clawed your way right to the top."

"Of course I did, Stuart." I'm so gracious. Never mind the fact that I save my wild side for the Swan and the other bars and clubs I frequent in the city, not the office. "You think a son of Harlan Pierce would leave an opportunity on the table?"

Stuart guffaws, his face pink from drinking, his tie already loosened. "Not for an instant." His buddies take turns shaking my hand and murmuring their congrats. The official announcement hasn't been made yet, but word is out.

Is it ever.

Once they've finished their little display of loyalty, Stuart finally notices Melody. In the skin tight red gown she's wearing, it's impossible to overlook her, but Stuart is the kind of ass who likes to play women for second-class citizens. To him, she's window dressing.

Like you're any better. A twinge of guilt arcs across my chest. I'm not any better than Stuart. In the game I've been playing for the past ten years, women are nothing more than pawns, entertainment.

And that's the way it's going to stay.

Stuart's eyes practically pop out of his head as he lustily scans up and down Melody's body, all the way from her cleavage down to her stilettos. "Well, hello there," he says, his tone leaving nothing to the imagination.

"Hello," Melody says icily. She's not much for fat older men, even if they happen to be wealthy. Not when she can go after younger billionaires like me. I'm a prince compared to Stuart.

Stuart juts his chin at me. "This guy giving you trouble, young lady?"

Melody gives him a thin smile that barely disguises her disgust. "Oh, no. Not at *all*."

Her tone is cutting, but Stuart laughs indulgently. "You're a fiery one, aren't you?"

I'm about to step in and defuse the situation with some witty remark that will steer Stuart back to the bar, but the music fades and stops. My father has stepped up onto the stage.

"Good evening," he says, the same winning smile that I've inherited plastered across his face. All around me people set down their plates of expensive hors d'oeuvres to applaud in acknowledgement.

"Gotta go," I whisper to Melody. I set my champagne glass down on a waiter's empty tray, and start making my way through the maze of tables as my father addresses the gathering.

My timing is perfect. I reach the stage as he says, "...so it's with great pride that I announce that my son, Christian Pierce, has officially been named Senior Vice President in charge of Pierce Industries' Entertainment Division."

A thrilled smile is painted across my lips as I climb the short set of stairs to join my father on the podium, but below the surface, I'm jumping out of my skin. My heartbeat pulses in my ears. I can never tell if my father does these things because he thinks I can handle the business or because he wants more control. At least when he's in control, he can still make sure I don't screw it up.

As if the fact that I spend most nights out on the town has any impact on my ability to manage my affairs at Pierce Industries. Harlan Pierce shouldn't have any problem with that lifestyle. It's the same one he's been leading for years.

At least when this grandiose announcement is over, I can make a hasty exit and get on with my night. At the Swan maybe, or back at my place. Maybe with Melody. I haven't tapped her yet, and I'm in the mood for someone frisky tonight.

Onstage, in front of everyone else, he pulls me in for a hug, and I scan his eyes searching for a sign that this is genuine. Looks real enough to me, but you never know.

"Congratulations, son," he says into my ear, and I clasp his arm above his elbow and grin back at him. Then it's my turn to speak to the assembly.

I take the microphone from his hand. "Thank you," I say easily, as if I was born to do this. "I'll do my best to make you proud, Dad." I wink at a woman standing near the stage in a dress with a plunging neckline as the crowd lets out a communal *awwww*. "With that said, don't let us interrupt your evening. Let's all get back to celebrating!"

The crowd bursts into another round of applause, and I turn to shake my father's hand once again. In moments, we're both making our way back through the crowd: my father heading to his table, and me to the nearest exit.

3

QUINN

I'm soaked to the skin, my clothes so wet it doesn't matter that it's raining anymore. The real bitch of the situation is the giant suitcase I'm hauling. It gets heavier with every step, and I'm starting to wonder if I *needed* all the shit I stuffed inside it back in Colorado. Most of my furniture went into a storage unit, while everything from Derek went directly into the dumpster. What's in the suitcase is the cream of the crop.

Maybe it would be better to set it down on the sidewalk and walk away, a case of finders, keepers. Everything in there, in some way or another, reminds me of Derek, of Colorado, of everything going wrong.

But I can't leave it. Best case scenario, someone picks through it and finds another use for what's inside. Worst case scenario, my unidentified large black suitcase causes a terrorism panic. Not the best way to make my debut in New York City, if you ask me.

At least it's a warm summer rain.

I stop at another intersection and squint up at the street sign. Three more blocks, and then I'll be at the new place. Carolyn assured me that it was absolutely fine to stay as long as I wanted. Her old roommate, Jessica, went to Europe to be the queen or princess or something of some tiny country there. Lucky for me, Carolyn decided loneliness isn't her style.

We'll be great roommates. I'm looking forward to things being a little closer to how they were in college. Back then, life wasn't nearly so complicated, and I hadn't been taken for a ride by a jackass fiancé.

It would be a plus, however, if I could get there before it's completely dark out. I'm not one hundred percent confident that drivers will notice me in my all-black clothing, what with the rain. Even if the sun were out, it would be hidden well below the buildings by now.

I'm traveling at a snail's pace, dragging the suitcase behind me. Silver lining? I get to check out a lot of the local restaurants and shops. An outfit in a boutique catches my eye, and for half a second I consider going in to look more closely. I catch a glimpse of my reflection in the window. I look more like a drowned rat than a PR specialist rising through the ranks at Holden Reputation Management, Inc., which is my profession when I'm not carting my belongings through the streets of New York in a rainstorm like an idiot who doesn't know how to hail a cab.

I laugh out loud at the reflection. That's how my day has gone.

Two and a half blocks to go.

For whatever reason, traffic is picking up. I thought I was

doing myself a favor by flying in after rush hour, but it's starting to look like it's always rush hour in this city. It's Thursday night, and people have places to *go*.

I cross through another intersection. *Two more blocks*. My arms ache from pulling the suitcase. Thank God I've been lifting some weights at the gym, or else I'd be hurting.

I distract myself from the burn by looking into the shops and restaurants on this block—there's a sushi place I might want to check out later—then step up to another intersection and wait for the light. A guy out for a jog—*really*?—darts around me and crosses against the light, which looks like a total suicide mission to me.

He's picked the wrong moment. A cab driver has to slam on the brakes at the last second to avoid hitting him. My heart leaps into my throat. Shit, that was *close*! There's a cacophony of horns honking and shouting.

Jogger Man never even turns his head, keeps on going down the sidewalk, totally unfazed.

Jesus. I like to take the occasional risk now and then—for instance, having my job transferred to New York City, despite only having visited it once a few years ago—but getting nailed by *any* kind of vehicle is not something I'm going to risk. Especially after my luck with the cab driver earlier.

I'm still recovering from the near-miss I witnessed when the light changes. I look both ways before I step off the curb, the wheels of my suitcase rattling on the concrete behind me.

God that was *such* a close call.

I'm halfway across the street when my suitcase catches on

something, jerking me backward. I give it a sharp tug. It doesn't come free. What the hell?

Rolling my eyes—is this day ever going to give me a break—I turn to look at what happened. Did one of the wheels break, or...?

Nope. One of the wheels has jammed. Right into a crack in the New York City asphalt.

Seriously.

I wrench the handle of the suitcase with my newly toned arms, but it doesn't budge. Underneath the sheen of the rain, beads of sweat start to collect on my hairline. The cars are awfully close, and I do not want to cause a huge scene when the light changes back again.

A glance at the walk sign tells me I don't have much time—the thing has already turned red, the hand flashing at me and the seconds counting down. Ten. Nine. Eight...

How is this thing *so* stuck? I try a different angle, pulling it to the side, and it moves a fraction of an inch.

"Shit, shit, *shit*," I say under my breath, yanking harder with every word.

I hear moving on the street, an engine revving, I glance up again at the surrounding cars, realizing in an instant that the light has changed. An SUV is barreling toward me, making a left-hand turn, the driver on the phone, not looking.

One gasping breath, one last powerful pull on the suitcase, and then I jump out of the way of the SUV, barely making it to safety.

My suitcase doesn't.

The SUV connects with my Samsonite with a dull thud. The upside is that the wheel is no longer stuck in the crack anymore. The downside is that the top pops open, sending clothes and books and shoes in every direction.

Like the jogger, the driver of the SUV keeps going as I stand on the curb, staring after him, my mouth hanging open in disbelief.

I get lots of pitying looks, but nobody stops their cars. Some of them try not to drive over anything intentionally, but I'll have to wait for the light to change before I can salvage anything.

A hand on my elbow startles me out of my dumbfounded thoughts, and I jerk away reflexively, only afterward turning to look into the most gorgeous set of blue eyes I have *ever* seen in my entire life.

The sight of them sends a shiver down my spine and at once I find it hard to breathe.

I forget all about the suitcase.

4

CHRISTIAN

At first, I don't see anything but how hot the woman is, how shapely her body is beneath her black tank top and yoga pants, how slick she looks in the rain, how her toned muscles flex as she tugs at the...

Is that a *suitcase*?

A woman who's going to pull a suitcase like that anywhere in this city instead of hailing a cab has to be a badass.

She looks over her shoulder at something and her eyes widen in panic. I can see the whites even in the dusky light of this cloudy evening, and something inside me shifts.

What are you thinking? Get off your ass and help her!

What *have* I been thinking? Am I that much of a douche? I scramble to the side of the car and push the door open, tuxedo be damned.

"Where are you—?" calls my driver, Louis, over his shoulder, but I slam the door shut behind me and start running.

I'm too late.

Some asshole driving an SUV that's obviously too much for him to handle makes a left turn with the light, but he doesn't look long enough to see that there's a gorgeous woman standing in the middle of the street. At the last second—holy *shit*, the *last* second—she jumps out of the way, but the suitcase gets nailed. Things go flying all over the intersection.

In typical New York City fashion, life moves on as soon as people realize that it was a suitcase that got hit and not a human being. Its owner stands on the street corner, her mouth parted slightly, watching as people drive over the contents of the bag.

I don't want to shout to get her attention, but by the time I'm close enough to speak to her, I can see she's still in shock.

I'd be pretty out of sorts if my suitcase had exploded all over a big city intersection. Then again, I can't see that happening—I have people to take care of that kind of thing. I don't handle my own luggage.

I reach out my hand and touch her arm, and she jerks away from me, surprised. Then, just as quickly, she turns to face me.

She's beautiful.

It doesn't matter that her hair is a mess, strands escaping from the bun on top of her head to stick against her face. It doesn't matter that she's not wearing any makeup, as far as I can tell. It doesn't matter that it's a dark and stormy night—her eyes are jade green, luminous, and the depth I see there takes the breath right out of my lungs.

My first instinct is to kiss her wet, full lips, but the feeling that comes right on its heels is that she's dangerous.

A woman with those lips, those eyes—she could do serious damage.

But I'm here to help, and so it only takes me a moment to decide what to say. Men like me are never caught off-guard, never threatened, we're only confident and charming as hell.

I point down the street to where her suitcase is resting on the yellow lines. "Is that yours?" I grin at her like we're conspirators, and pink color rises to her cheeks.

"Yeah," she says with a small smile and a shake of her head. "That asshole destroyed it."

"He did," I say, surveying the intersection. "But you can salvage some of it. I'll help you collect it when the light changes."

"You don't have to do that," she says, but when I look back, I see she hasn't taken her eyes off my face.

"I'm already out in the rain." I pitch my voice a little lower but she doesn't respond, her breasts rising underneath the tank top with her deep inhale.

"So is my stuff," she says matter-of-factly. "It's probably ruined. But I'm not going to leave it out here like a bunch of garbage."

"If you wanted to leave it, I could send someone to pick it up later."

Now her expression turns quizzical. "Send someone? Why would you do that? And—how?" She scans my clothes, and then her eyes lock back on mine. "Are you one of those ultra-wealthy men who has people for everything?"

I don't bother lying. Most of the city knows me by reputation, if not by sight. "As a matter of fact, I am."

She gives me a long look, then seems to make a decision. "I've got to at least get some of it."

The walk signal turns back on. "Quick," I say, "this is our chance."

We dart out into the intersection, stuffing our arms with sopping clothes, flattened books, and mismatched pairs of shoes. When the light changes again, we both sprint back to the curb, where she bursts out laughing.

"This is a hell of a way to start things off."

"What things?" I say, grinning at her pure, musical laughter.

"Living in New York."

I put my armload of stuff onto the sidewalk and spread my arms wide. "Welcome to the city!"

"Damn right."

It takes three trips to get the majority of her stuff back to the curb, and then I go after the suitcase. The zipper is busted, but it can hold her things for the time being. She piles it all in, then ties it shut with a pair of pantyhose.

Straightening back up, she looks at me, eyes alight. "Thanks for helping me out. It's the first time since—" Then she shakes her head. "Never mind. Thank you." She extends a hand. "Quinn Campbell."

"Christian Pierce," I say. When our hands touch there's a

kind of electric charge, and I resist the urge to keep holding on. "Let me give you a ride. My driver is waiting right over there." I gesture to where Louis has double-parked.

"I'm all right," she says, holding up a hand. "I'm a block away from my new place. I'll be all right." With that, she turns away, pulling the beat-up suitcase behind her.

"You sure?"

"Completely," she says with a final glance over her shoulder, and I see the hint of a smile on her face. After that, she never turns back.

I watch her until she's lost behind traffic and people.

I'll probably never see Quinn Campbell again.

What happens next surprises me, the feeling rising in my chest.

It's regret.

5

QUINN

Carolyn opens the door, takes one look at me, and screeches, "Q! Why didn't you *call* for a *ride*?"

I burst out laughing—I can't help it. This entire traveling experience has been so ridiculous that it's the only one way to respond. Carolyn ushers me into the entryway of her apartment—now *my* apartment, too—and looks from me to my pantyhose-tied suitcase with her mouth hanging open.

"What the hell happened to you?" she says after my laughter has died out.

"Oh, Care," I say, putting my hands to my forehead. "I landed at LaGuardia and got a cab, but the driver turned out to be a total psycho, so I made him let me out early. And then the suitcase got stuck in the street—"

"*How*?"

"That's not even the worst thing! Some idiot in an SUV ran over it with his car!"

"And you didn't call the *police*?" she interjects, her voice getting even louder.

"No!" I shout back at her, a tinge of hysteria in my voice. "I didn't call anybody! I didn't even get the cab driver's name!"

"Oh, my God," Carolyn says, before springing into action. "You can't stand there in wet clothes. Come here. No, don't worry about the carpet. Follow me."

I stop only to peel off my shoes and socks, tucking the soaked pieces of fabric into the palm of one of my hands.

Carolyn leads me through the entry hallway and across the living room, then down another hallway, speaking as we go. "This is where the bedrooms are. Mine is down on the right, and yours is right here." She opens a door, and I step into a second bedroom that's easily twice as large as the master bedroom in my house in Colorado.

Yeah, Carolyn is *loaded*. It's not like I'm a slouch in the money-making department, but I can't touch the kind of trust fund that Care and the majority of her rich friends have.

I follow her across the plush carpeting of the bedroom that's now mine. It smells freshly cleaned and the bed is already made up with a tasteful comforter and throw pillows. "You didn't need to go to so much trouble," I say, taking it all in.

"It was absolutely no trouble at all," says Carolyn, a little formally, as if we didn't live together for two years back when experimenting with frat boys was all the rage.

"No, really, Care," I say as she precedes me into a large bathroom. The shower is glass-enclosed and fancy as hell with one of those rainwater shower heads. "It means a lot. Thank you."

She smiles at me, and her whole face lights up. Carolyn is one of those people who comes off as sweet even when she's acting tough. The heart can hardly handle it when she's being her regular nice self. Then she gets another glimpse of my soaking clothes and gestures to the towels that hang from brass hooks on the wall near the shower.

"Towels are here," she says. "My cleaning service keeps the bathrooms stocked with shampoo, conditioner, and body wash, but if you don't like any of it, let me know and I'll have them replace it with your brand. There's a robe hanging on the back of the door. I'll get you some of my things to wear once you're out."

The tension of the day is leaving my shoulders, and I haven't stepped into the shower yet.

Carolyn bustles toward the door, then turns back. "Quinn?"

"Yeah?"

"Are you having other clothes sent? Or was everything in your suitcase?"

I let out a little sigh. "I wasn't going to send anything else."

She nods once. "If you don't mind—while you're in here, I'll separate the clothes and set them aside for the cleaner. We can shop tomorrow, if you want—there's plenty of my stuff to borrow from in the meantime."

"Fine by me. I always wanted to go on a New York City shopping spree." This isn't exactly true. I've never thought about going on a New York City shopping spree until this moment, but Carolyn brightens at the idea.

"Enjoy," she says, then pulls the bathroom door shut behind her.

Thirty minutes later, I emerge clean and fresh, my hair dried and brushed out into shining dark waves. There's a lot less tension on my scalp now that my hair isn't twisted into a heavy bun.

Carolyn has stocked the closet in my bedroom with several outfits. On the bed, she laid out a plain pink tank with matching lounge pants.

She gets me.

I wander out into the living room to find her curled up on the couch, a mug of tea in her hand.

"You look nice," she says when she sees me, then holds up the mug. "Want some?"

"I'm all right," I say, then flop down across from her. Her air conditioning is running full-blast against the July heat, but there are soft blankets placed strategically on the arms of the couch and across the back. I pull one over my legs as Carolyn considers me.

"You've had a day," she says finally, and I hear the invitation to talk in her voice.

"I've had a *month*."

"Ugh," Carolyn says, looking down. "I'm sorry about all that with Derek. That's...awful. We don't have to talk about it if you don't want to."

"It's—" A lump comes to my throat. The betrayal is still so fresh and raw. "He's a dick. I'm better off without him."

"You so are!" Carolyn looks back at me, then changes the subject. "Looks like New York City gave you quite the welcome."

"It was *not* what I was expecting when I got on the plane this morning," I say, then cover my eyes with my hands. "My suitcase got run over by a car! And the driver didn't even stop! Tell me not everyone in New York City is that crazy."

"Not everyone in New York City is that crazy."

"Not if the cab driver is any indication."

"What was his problem?" Carolyn stretches out her legs onto the matching ottoman. "I haven't heard too many cab horror stories since I moved here. Then again—"

"Your friends have drivers?" I laugh at the thought of having a driver. Like Christian Pierce, the smoking hot guy in the tuxedo who appeared out of nowhere when my suitcase exploded. "I met a guy with a driver today."

"Did you?" Carolyn's brow wrinkles. "Where?"

"On the street corner. Wait. That doesn't sound right." We both laugh, and then I tell her the story of the man in the tuxedo rushing to my aid, only it was too late. I leave out the fact that looking into his eyes made my entire body heat up. I leave out the fact that when I turned away from him, I wanted to march right back and ask him for a date.

What was stopping you? The thought rises in the back of my mind, but I swat it away. *Remember Derek? No way are you jumping headfirst into dating on your first day.*

"—wearing a tux, Care," I finish.

"Did you get his number?"

"No," I say, then laugh. "No way. I am not on the market. I got his name though. Christian."

"Christian *Pierce*?" Carolyn shrieks.

"Yes?" How the hell does she know him?

My friend laughs so hard tears come to the corners of her eyes.

"Carolyn, what—"

"Oh, my God, this is too much. Remember back in college, how we used to talk about our friends from school? You know who Jess is, but Chris—that's short for Christian. Christian Pierce and I have been friends for a long time."

It all hits me at once. Carolyn knows the mystery man with the stunning blue eyes. My guess is, they run in the same social circle.

The truth is that when I walked away from him, I thought I'd never see him again. Why would I run into a guy like that at work, or at my apartment? Why would I run into him in a city this big, when I'm a regular girl running away from Colorado?

Looks like the city got smaller.

6

CHRISTIAN

Quinn is burned into my brain.

Friday morning at the Pierce Industries building, and it's time to move into my new corner office on the eighteenth floor, where the entertainment division is headquartered. My assistant brought down most of my things yesterday before she left for the day, so all there is to do now is to look through my desk and make sure I haven't left anything behind.

I open all the drawers.

Empty. Every one.

Not a single trace of me remains in this office.

"Feeling sentimental?"

My father leans against the doorway, his Italian suit tailored perfectly to his lean frame.

"For this old place?" I say with a grin, standing up from behind the desk. "Not at all. Bigger and better things."

"That's my boy," he says wryly, but there's an undercurrent of approval there. A hot spike of resentment burns through my chest. All those years that he thought my brother walked on water...

To cover it up, I smile even wider, meeting him at the doorway. "Monthly board meeting?"

"Business as usual," he says with a little sigh, even though I know he loves board meetings. The board of directors at Pierce Industries is largely decorative. It's a private company, but my father thought it would give his decisions more legitimacy if he could collect opinions from the board before he announced them.

Not that they ever sway him. He likes to throw his weight around. Dear old dad is a devious bastard like that.

You're not much better.

And then another thought, hard on its heels:

What would Quinn Campbell think?

To cover it, I smile wider at my father, let him clap me on the back, and then walk with him to the elevators. "Meetings of my own," I say, and then a car arrives, going down. I step in, but my father steps back. He's going up.

Isn't that always how it is?

The door slides shut behind me, and I put a hand to my head.

Why the hell would I possibly care what Quinn Campbell thinks? She's some woman I met for twenty minutes in the rain yesterday, not the love of my life.

There's never going to be a love of my life.

It's not in the cards for Christian Pierce.

Not now, not ever.

Because that would mean...

I shake my head sharply. I'm not going to think about it.

What I need to do is focus on my job. On my friends. I have plans for a group to go to the Swan tonight. I'm bringing Melody. She doesn't work for Pierce Industries. Partners have been known to bring women who are "temping as assistants" with them to the gala to liven things up.

It worked.

But the main thing I care about is that when I end things with Melody—and I will end things, in three dates or less—it won't become an issue at the office. She gets what she wants. I get the distraction I want. No workplace drama.

Except in my own head.

I don't want to go to the Swan with Melody. I want to go back in time and ask Quinn Campbell if she'll be my date instead.

I'd break the rules for her.

No. I won't.

The thought chills me to the core, and for the hundredth time today, I wonder how the hell a woman I saw for twenty minutes has such a hold over me.

It's not *love*. I'm not in love with her. I *want* her. I'm intrigued by her. I want to know more about her. I want to know what made her decide to drag that massive suitcase through the rain in SoHo. I want to know what made her flinch when I touched her arm. I want to know why she was more worried about her things becoming litter than about saving any of them. Where did she come from, that when her life was splattered all over a New York City intersection, she didn't even cry?

Maybe she's tough.

Or maybe there's more to know about her.

I could look her up. I give Stephanie, my assistant, a nod as I go past her and into my office. No. I dismiss the idea. I'm not going to go chasing some woman all over the city to...

To what? Take her on three dates, and then leave her behind like all the rest?

Something tells me it won't be that easy.

But I can't afford for it to be difficult.

I absolutely cannot allow those kinds of complications into my life, because if I were to fall in love...

I could fall in love with her.

I take a deep breath and let it out through my nose. This is crazy. This kind of thinking—it's going to get me into trouble.

Those captivating green eyes have sucked me in. The confident way she stood, the way she spoke, imprinted itself on my mind, and I can't forget her.

Quinn Campbell.

"Stop," I say out loud, bringing my hand down on the

surface of my desk, and moments later Stephanie appears at the door.

"Did you need something, Mr. Pierce?"

"No, Stephanie. Actually—" I wrack my brain for a plausible request, something to hide the fact that something is bothering me, hide the fact that I'm not my usual carefree cocky self. "Give me a rundown of my schedule today."

"Absolutely," she says, looking down at a notepad nestled in the crook of her arm. "In fifteen minutes, there's a department update meeting. At lunch, you're scheduled to go out with..."

I'm looking at her, trying my damnedest to pay attention, but those eyes...

My phone buzzes in my pocket and I pull it out, desperate for a distraction. "Give me a minute, Stephanie."

At first, I don't understand the message on my screen.

It's from Carolyn.

Why didn't you tell me you met my new roommate? ;)

She had mentioned a new roommate, someone moving in this week from out in Colorado. A college roommate. I can't remember the name, but...

It hits me like a Mack truck.

The suitcase.

The rain.

Carolyn's neighborhood.

Quinn Campbell is Carolyn's roommate.

7

QUINN

Friday morning comes quietly. I'd imagined that living in New York City would be like sticking my head into a waterfall of pure noise—the city that never sleeps, and all that—but Carolyn lives a charmed life. Her apartment is on the sixth floor of the building and the walls and windows are thick, blocking out all but the most insistent street noise.

I'm stretched out in the queen-size bed, luxuriating in the soft sheets that Carolyn's made up the bed with, when my phone blares its ringtone from the bedside table, sending my heart rate through the roof.

"Shit!" I blurt into the shattered quiet of the room and fumble for the phone, snatching it up before it goes to voicemail. "Hello?"

"Ms. Campbell?" It's a man, but I can't identify the deep voice. A wild hope that maybe it's Christian Pierce thunders through me. Christian, the man with the stunning eyes, the chiseled jaw I kept seeing in my dreams last night. I don't know how he got my number, but—

"Yeah. Yes. That's me," I say, putting my hand to my chest.

"This is Greg Porter of Porter Plumbing," rumbles the voice on the other end of the line. Oh, Jesus, I forgot all about the message I left at the first plumbing company that popped up in a Google search. The realtor had someone come out and shut off the water, so the pipes aren't *actively* leaking—at least, I hope he's not calling to say there's been a flood.

"Hi, Greg," I say smoothly, my PR training kicking in. "Was Sherrie able to let you into the house?"

"Yes," he says, but there's a hitch in his voice that tells me all is not well. "But Ms. Campbell..."

"Lay it on me, Greg. What's the deal with my basement?"

"The situation is going to involve more than pipe repair."

"Okay?"

"The water wasn't shut off quickly enough to prevent any damage to the drywall and the carpeting." His sigh comes over the line clear as a bell. "It's only lucky that you've moved out most of the furniture and possessions. Look, Ms. Campbell, we can fix the pipes, but you're going to need a contractor to come down here and take a look at the drywall. At the very least, the carpet will need to be professionally cleaned, and with the amount of time the water's been sitting—"

It occurs to me that Sherrie had the water turned off. She didn't have it *removed* from the basement. Shit.

"I understand. Are you able to do the repairs on the pipes, at least?"

He takes a second to answer, and my heart sinks. What the hell *happened* at my house? I turned the keys over to the realtor two weeks ago so that I could have stagers come in. Sherrie assured me that if I was out and everything was properly arranged, the house would go much faster. It's like Colorado has me clamped in its jaw and doesn't want to let go. It's practically begging me to fly back and sort all of this out by myself.

I grit my teeth. I'm *not* going back there. Not for anything.

"Yep," he says, and from the way he says the word I get the impression that he's standing in several inches of water in the basement of the house that shouldn't be mine any longer. "We can get that squared away by five, six o'clock tonight."

"Thanks, Greg," I say. "I'll speak to someone about the drywall."

"That's probably the best idea."

I disconnect the call and flop back onto my plush, firm pillows.

Go ahead, universe. Hit me with it. I can take it.

Half an hour later, I'm riding the elevator down to the lobby of Carolyn's building—*my* building—wearing a summery dress on loan from her closet, my hair piled on top of my head in an elaborate bun that looks more complicated than it is. I'm meeting Carolyn for lunch in three hours. In the meantime, I'm shopping.

I browse some of the boutiques I saw last night on my rainy trek through SoHo, treasuring it every time I come out of an air-conditioned clothing store into the gentle morning sunlight. The rest of my life might be waterlogged, but this —this is perfect.

Until my phone buzzes in my purse as I'm making my way back toward the sushi restaurant I wanted to try. It's not far from the building where Carolyn works—one of her favorites, she said when I told her about it last night.

"Hello!" I lilt into the phone, my mind on a coral dress that's inside one of my shopping bags. It's going to look sharp as hell under a blazer for work, and classy but hot for a night out. Not that I'm planning any nights out. I'm perfectly content to watch Lifetime movies with Carolyn every night until forever.

"Quinn Campbell?"

"This is she."

"This is Bennett Walker from HRM. I'm calling to check in —have you arrived in the city yet?"

"Yes, I have!" I say. A cab pulls slowly up to the curb next to me, and anxiety spikes down my spine. Is it that psycho coming for his revenge? A guy in a suit jogs up to the car and hops inside. My pulse slows.

"Ms. Campbell?" says Bennett Walker. I must have missed something in my distraction about the cab.

"Sorry about that—my attention was on something here. What did you say?"

"No problem. I said that I hoped the city was treating you well."

I can't help but laugh at that one, but there's no reason to burden my new boss with the story of my arrival. "It's wonderful. Thanks for asking."

"The reason I'm calling," he says, "is that there's been a change here that's going to affect your job description."

My heart plummets into my shoes. Jesus Christ. Am I getting fired? Demoted? It would be right in line with everything else that's happened, with the one exception of Carolyn's awesome apartment.

"We've brought on a high-profile client. It's a new account," Walker continues. "Instead of coming in on the associate level, we'd like to bump you up to an executive of reputation management. Obviously we'll have a new salary offer commensurate with the increased responsibility."

"You're giving me a *promotion*?" I say, unable to keep the relief out of my voice.

"You come *highly* recommended from the Boulder branch, and we need someone experienced to handle this client. All of the other people we'd tap are maxed out on accounts, so your transfer is coming at the perfect time."

"That...sounds great!" I say. Maybe New York City *isn't* going to be a disaster.

"See you on Monday, Ms. Campbell," Walker says. "Enjoy yourself this weekend."

"I will. Goodbye!"

"Who was that?"

The voice comes from directly behind me, and I whirl around, coming face to face with Carolyn.

"My new job," I say, giving her a quick hug. "They promoted me."

"*Already*?"

"I know! Something about a new client? I'm not going to argue."

"You know what we need to do?" Carolyn says, hooking her arm in mine and tugging me toward the door of the restaurant. "Celebrate. We're going out tonight. To the Purple Swan."

8

CHRISTIAN

It's a typical Friday night at the Purple Swan. Everyone's energy is high, incandescent somehow, and even the wait staff seems to be in on it. They're practically running from the kitchens to the tables to the bars and back, and though the Swan is too high class to overbook, there aren't many seats sitting empty around the linen-covered tables.

But the noise is giving me a headache.

I look across the table at the two empty seats, an anomaly on a night like tonight—but Jax Hunter, one of my closest friends in New York, bailed on me tonight, along with his wife, Cate. They're usually excellent company.

I don't want company tonight.

I want to go back to my penthouse, alone, where there's no one else at all, and stay in the den until I'm too tired to stay awake anymore. The silence would be a blessing. The darkness would stop the pounding in my head.

Normally, I'd fantasize about being at my penthouse alone, but tonight I haven't been able to stop myself. I'm imagining Quinn Campbell's lithe body tucked next to me on my leather sectional, her breasts rising and falling under a skintight tank top. She smelled good even in the rain, like pure soap with an undercurrent of fresh flowers.

But Christian Pierce *never* bails on Friday night.

There's no slipping out the back entrance alone when Melody is in the picture, at any rate, and Christ, is she ever in the picture.

The black dress she's wearing is cut so low in the front that I swear I keep catching glimpses of her belly button, and her makeup is heavy and dark, making her gray eyes stand out in sharp contrast to her deep red lips.

"Where's your mind at, Christian?" she murmurs to me during a break in the conversation. Two of my friends are out tonight—Todd and Jeffrey—and they have both brought along women who I've never met. The four of them seem to be getting along famously. Meanwhile, I've been chiming in on autopilot, flashing a half smile I don't mean, to cover up the fact that I'm not paying much attention.

Apparently, it didn't fool Melody.

"Your dress," I say. It's not entirely a lie.

It's not entirely the truth, either.

She gives me a little grin, cocking her head to the side. "Are you sure that's all?"

I dart my eyes down to her cleavage. "How could I possibly be thinking of anything else?"

"You're not looking very closely for someone who loves this dress."

"I wouldn't want you to think I only care about clothing."

"That's *right*," she says, her sensual tone wrapping around the back of my neck. "It's what's *under* the dress that's captured your imagination."

Melody's usually seductive voice does nothing to alleviate my headache, which is growing by the minute.

It does nothing to take my mind off Quinn Campbell, who has invaded my innermost thoughts and taken up permanent residence since the moment I first saw her. It doesn't help that she's Carolyn's roommate. She's so *close.* All I'd need to do to get her number is send one text message to Carolyn.

When she first texted me about her roommate, I responded casually, lightly, laughing it off. *What a hilarious coincidence, I can't believe it, that's New York City for you.*

The lightning shooting through my veins implies this is more than a meeting by happenstance. Even if it is a coincidence, it has the potential to be so *much* more.

You can never *go there.*

Even Melody's alluring come-on can't shake her out of my mind. For once, my endless well of charming quips fails me completely. I lean over and kiss the side of her neck to hide that I'm barely responding to her, even though she's pulling out all the stops. Melody smells, oddly, like baby powder. When I pull back, she's looking at me with heated eyes, lustful eyes. *I have to get out of this, I can't take her home with me, I don't want to.*

"Fancy meeting you here," says a voice, crystal clear, from the other side of the table. Relief washes over me as I turn away from Melody—the comment was obviously meant for me, and it would be rude as hell to ignore it.

Carolyn stands near the two empty seats, looking great in something short and midnight blue, but it's the person behind her who immediately consumes my full attention.

Quinn Campbell stands confidently in the middle of the hustle and bustle of the Purple Swan, a complete knockout in a structured red gown, her dark hair falling in loose curls around her face, over her shoulders. I want more than anything to stand up, walk around the table, and run my hands through it right now before I kiss her.

Our eyes lock and her mouth quirks in a strange little smile. I'm dying to know what's going on inside her head, dying to touch her skin under her gown, dying to know everything about her. The energy between us crackles across the empty space.

"Quinn Campbell," I call across the table, laughter on my lips, a smile on my face that keeps everything hidden under the surface. "Tell me that suitcase made it home."

"Of *course* it did," she says in a saucy tone, sidling up to stand next to Carolyn. "This wasn't in it, though. I bought this especially for our girls' night."

I raise my eyebrows. "You can't waste that gown on a couple of seats at the bar."

Carolyn pats the back of the empty chairs. "Are these taken?"

"Now they are," Quinn says, lowering herself gracefully into the chair across from me. "Quinn Campbell," she says, looking around the table. "Who are all you jokers?"

Carolyn laughs, sitting down beside her, and everyone else joins in.

Everyone but Melody.

Out of the corner of my eye, I catch a glimpse of her face. Her eyes are narrowed, ruby lips pressed together, and she's gripping the edge of the table like it might float away.

This is not her night.

9

QUINN

I get up early on Monday morning. I have to be prepared, even if my mind is still reeling from that evening at the Swan. Still, everything has to be perfect on my first day at HRM. The promotion has raised the stakes. Not only will I be working at HRM's world headquarters, I'll be handling a "high-profile client." I'm not sure what that means yet in New York City terms—I'm certain it will be on another level from the clients I managed in Boulder—but this is going to be *big.*

My nerves started kicking in last night. I don't have a fall-back plan. The moment my house in Colorado sells, there'll be nowhere to run back to if this job relocation goes south. I guess I could always try transferring back—but no, I couldn't. If I'm not the massive success my previous supervisors predicted I would be, I could find myself jobless in New York, relying fully on Carolyn's mercy.

For the first time in a long time, I don't have a boyfriend—or a fiancé—to serve as my safety net.

There's no choice but to be a smash hit at HRM from here on out. It was one thing to be a big fish in a small pond back in Colorado, but I'm going to need to be incredible if I'm going to succeed in New York. I can already sense the competition in the air. People here are bloodthirsty when it comes to climbing the career ladder. One wrong move, and you can go tumbling all the way down to the concrete, never to be heard from again.

The job isn't the least of it.

I might be a little bit obsessed with Christian Pierce.

When I saw him at the Swan, I wanted to walk around the table and push that other woman out of the seat next to him. What's the story behind those eyes? I couldn't work up the courage to ask Carolyn more about him for the rest of the weekend. Something is making me hesitate. The last thing I want is to seem like some flighty idiot who latches on to the first shiny object she sees, even if that object happens to be a living, breathing man with an incredible body and eyes that keep me awake at night.

I can't get him out of my head. The sexy half-smile, the way he's so effortlessly charming, and his eyes...there's something deeper there, a secret he's not sharing.

Or maybe not. Maybe he is exactly what he seems—a billionaire playboy with too much money, a cocky attitude, and a body that can net him any woman he wants. Maybe I want him to be more complicated so I have an excuse to be intrigued.

Stop, I tell myself firmly as I apply a coat of mascara to my eyelashes. Makeup first—sharp and neutral and wholly professional—then my hair. I spent an extra ten minutes in the shower making sure my legs were shaved to perfection. *You cannot have your attention overtaken by a man right now.*

Not even if that man *is* Christian Pierce.

Did I imagine it, or was he looking at me with the same intensity I felt? The woman he was with—Melody, I think it was—didn't look very happy about the little back-and-forth we had going between us when Carolyn and I were first sitting down.

Whatever. From what little I have heard from Carolyn, Christian dates like it's going out of style.

My heart turns over. There's another reason I should steer clear of him. From here on out, I'm only interested in men who give a shit about things like commitment.

And *honesty*.

Derek was the last bastard to get the chance at destroying my heart with bullshit like having a secret affair with my best friend. For an entire year.

I sweep my hair back into a flawless chignon, put on my new coral dress and a snappy blazer, slip my feet into nude high heels that make me look like a supermodel, and head out the door right on time, my phone and wallet tucked into an oversized purse that usually holds my laptop. On the off chance that HRM assigns me one today, I'm not going to want to haul two of them across the city.

I take the subway to Midtown, emerging into the bright July morning with a spring to my step and hope in my heart.

And Christian Pierce on my mind.

Bennett Walker turns out to be several inches shorter than I am, a concentrated ball of energy waiting to take on the day. He greets me as soon as I enter the building lobby. "Bennett Walker," he says, holding out his free hand. In the other hand, he carries a leather portfolio. "Everyone calls me Walker. Feel free."

"Quinn Campbell." He rocks up and down on the balls of his feet, always ready to speed off in a different direction.

"We're on the eighth and ninth floors," he says as he guides me across to the security station, where the men there create a new I.D. badge that I will need to access the elevators. "I'm glad you're here early. There are actually a couple of meetings already on your schedule for this morning."

"Orientation meetings?"

"Client meetings."

I don't let the shock show on my face, although I can't believe they're having me meet with clients on my first day. "Okay," I say as we wait for the next elevator car to arrive. "I'm assuming there will be some kind of briefing?"

"You're good, Campbell," Walker says with a grin on his face. "I can hardly tell you're rattled. The briefing is going to be —" He glances down at his wristwatch. "Right now. Buckle up."

10

CHRISTIAN

I don't care about what happened on Friday night.

My father *does*.

Color me shocked.

Melody was pissed about the way I talked to Quinn Campbell across the table when she showed up with Carolyn. She was angry when they sat down and furious that they stayed, and she didn't hide it very well.

To her credit, Quinn never seemed to let it affect her. She struck up conversations with Todd's and Jeff's dates and played off Carolyn's contributions to the conversation. By the time they polished off the last of their drinks—wine for Carolyn and vodka and Red Bull for Quinn—and gathered their clutch purses to go, Melody's fury was rolling off her in waves.

I hated to watch Quinn's back as she receded into the crowd. Why was I so drawn to her? Why can't I pinpoint the thing that kept my eyes laser-focused on her face, the curve of her shoulders, the neckline of her dress, for the rest of the night? Maybe it's how she radiates confidence like nobody I've ever seen. Maybe it's that she doesn't seem to be swept away by me. For once, I'm not in control.

It's not my favorite feeling.

I wasn't always this way, but ever since—

No.

I shove the thought out of my mind. I don't want to focus on those days. I don't want to focus on my brother, the party... any of it.

It has nothing to do with Quinn Campbell.

It has everything to do with Quinn Campbell, and you know it.

I run my hands down over my face, then try to force my attention back to my computer screen.

It doesn't work.

What's wrong with me? Quinn Campbell is a woman I cannot—absolutely *cannot*—afford to get involved with. I don't know how I'm so sure. I don't know how I can sense it. But I know that if Quinn Campbell gets too close to me, I won't be able to resist her. I won't be able to keep her from knowing the deepest parts of me.

Then she'll know my secret.

And *no one* can know my secret.

A meeting reminder pops up in the corner of my computer screen, and I push my chair away from my desk with infinite care to keep from slamming my fists against it. It's time to make my way to my father's office. He has summoned me to a meeting, and by the terse tone of his message, it'll be regarding the events of Friday night.

After Quinn and Carolyn took off, I sat next to a seething Melody, trying to defuse the tension with a few well-placed one-liners. She was having none of it, and my patience grew thin.

For the first time in a long time, I left the Swan before my friends.

It's been months—years, maybe—since I've taken a risk like that. Christian Pierce never bails. He's the life of the party. He's the last one to leave.

Not Friday night.

I had put down my glass—by then, I was getting by on water, that's how terrible the pain in my head was becoming —and stood up, waving away my friends' expressions of concern and shocked looks.

"Where you going, buddy?" Todd said, his voice too loud. His date cuddled up into his shoulder, and I knew that it wouldn't be long before he found his way to one of the Swan's hotel rooms to spend the rest of the night undressed with her. I wished for one moment that I had been able to leave with Quinn, take her back to my place and undress *her*, but that ship had sailed.

"Calling it a night," I said with a devilish smile that suggested I'd be doing otherwise, only not at the Swan. Let them think I was going to another exclusive club, or some dive bar or a hotel room somewhere.

I gracefully acknowledged their drunken chorus of good-byes, then tried to fade away into the crowd.

Melody followed.

For the most part, the throbbing music drowned her out, but I could hardly interject over her hissed accusations. "Chris!" I heard as I passed between two tables on the way to the back exit. "Who the hell was that—?"

"I'm headed home, Melody," I said loudly, my own voice ringing in my ears. "Do you want me to call a car for you?"

Her face turned an even darker shade of red at the suggestion that we wouldn't be riding home together. "Fuck you," she spat, her eyes narrowed, then whirled around and stalked off toward the restrooms.

I should have been home free then, but Melody changed her mind. I was nearly to the curb when she burst out of the back exit of the Swan.

"You're a man slut," she shouted, the slur in her words more obvious in the crystal silence of the side street. "Why did you bring me here?"

Too late, the paparazzi lurking ten feet away down the sidewalk registered in my mind. They make the rounds by the Swan in case anything sensational happens. Friday was their lucky night.

Melody was still trailing after me, stomping comically in a pair of stiletto heels that didn't deserve the punishment. "You're such a sick bastard!" she screamed.

I held both hands up, shaking my head. "Mel, you're drunk."

"I'm not *drunk*," she shouted, and the paparazzi came toward us then, cameras flashing, shutters clicking.

Louis pulled the Town Car up to the curve and I dove in to

the back seat, quickly shutting the door behind me, but not before they got a nice shot of Melody swinging her purse at me, her face contorted in rage.

I'm forcing myself not to roll my eyes at the memory when I breeze past my father's secretary and pull open the doors to his office, striding in with my back straight and my chin up. He's not a man who bestows pity points, so it's best to act as though I've done nothing wrong.

He looks up from his leather-bound business diary, an artifact from the ancient days of his youth, I assume, and cocks one eyebrow at me. "Interesting night you had on Friday, son."

"Can't argue with that."

The corners of his mouth turn up slightly, and he lets out a half-hearted sigh. "I can't say I haven't been in that position once or twice." He closes the diary and looks back up at me. "I'm not going to tell you how to spend your free time, Christian, but we need to make some changes when it comes to Pierce Industries."

"What kinds of changes?" I drop into a seat across from him, doing my best to look comfortable, doing my best to look like my heart isn't hammering against my rib cage.

"You have earned quite the reputation around the city as a man who enjoys the finer things in life. Food. Women. Drinks." Now he's openly smiling at me, and I smile back. It doesn't feel natural. I'm still waiting for the other shoe to drop. I'll always be waiting for that shoe to drop. "When it comes to your responsibilities here, we need to project an aura of..." His voice trails off as he searches for the appropriate word. "Respectability."

"I see."

"So I've hired a new PR firm to help you brush up on your image. It doesn't mean you stop frequenting your club. Work with them on creating some other opportunities to be photographed under other circumstances."

"Not a problem," I say with a smile, and my father nods.

I get up from my seat, torn in two. On the one hand, I'm relieved—my father approves of my choices. The thing with the paparazzi wasn't entirely my fault. On the other hand, I'm sick at heart. Because if I had been anyone else...

"I've scheduled their first meeting with you before lunch, at their offices," my father says as I turn to leave. "Have your driver take you over."

I give him a jaunty salute, then keep going.

"They've promised me they will assign you to the best reputation management expert they have on staff. Don't give them too much trouble, son."

11

QUINN

I'm drowning in pure adrenaline. That's why it takes me a full five minutes to process what Walker is telling me about the company. Multibillion-dollar corporation. Privately owned by the father, who has the majority vote for any decision. Grooming his son to one day take the reins of leadership. Playboy. Partier. Womanizer. I'm listening so closely to every word that comes out of his mouth that they divide themselves up into unintelligible chunks that take a few moments to resolve in my mind.

Wait.

Playboy?

Womanizer?

This sounds familiar.

"Wait," I say, cutting Walker off mid-sentence. We're halfway down the hall leading to my new office. Normally, I would take a lot of delight in relishing this moment—the first walk to the space representing how far I've climbed since graduating college—but my mind roils with all the various pressures competing for my attention. The need to excel at this job, no matter what. The way my house is still hanging around my neck, a weight I need to cast off before it drowns me. And Christian Pierce's eyes. "Did you tell me the name of the client? My mind is racing a little here."

"Pierce Industries."

My heart stops, then starts beating again.

"Pierce Industries," I repeat after him, testing the name out on my tongue. There's no way it's a coincidence.

"Yes," Walker barrels on, not breaking his stride. "Harlan Pierce reached out to us personally. This is a bit of a special assignment."

He stops in front of the doorway to my office and swings his arm out wide. It's huge, as far as offices go, and the view of the street below is stunning—but I don't see it. *Special assignment.* Jesus Christ. Where is he heading with this?

I step around Walker and into the office, heading straight for the desk. It's a glass, modern creation set off by a futuristic-looking chair for me on one side of it and two comfortable seats for clients and anyone I'll be managing. I assume I'll be managing someone, since I oversaw a team of three people back in Colorado.

It's like Walker hears my thoughts right through my skull.

"Now, usually we'd spend the first few weeks building out a team for you to manage client accounts. But Pierce Industries is such a heavy hitter that senior management has decided to dedicate a full-time person to them to begin with.

If they have other needs in the future, we can add more personnel, and you'll direct all those activities."

I keep my face perfectly composed when I reply, but my tongue is unwieldy in my mouth. "What are their needs currently?"

Walker holds out the portfolio that he's been carrying. I take it from him, the leather cool and smooth under my fingertips.

"Specialized reputation management." Okay—this is going to be a one-on-one job. I flip open the portfolio, and there on the cover page is a press photo of Christian, gazing into the camera with a cocky smile.

My stomach does a slow flip, and I swallow a sudden dryness that appears in my mouth.

It takes everything I have, but I force myself to scan the fact sheet. Right at the top, I find the reason why Pierce Industries is so interested in managing Christian's reputation. His father has put him in charge of their entertainment division, which is clearly a move made in advance of promoting him to CEO. One day, he's going to direct Pierce Industries in entirety. I know better than anyone that a person that visible needs the kind of PR management I can offer.

If, that is, I can slow my heart down to a normal level.

"Are they sending a representative?"

Walker shakes his head. "As far as I can tell, he's coming down personally to meet with you. Harlan Pierce was very explicit about his requirements—they want actionable items by the end of the week."

I nod once.

"Hey," Walker says in a comforting tone. "You can do this. You came highly recommended—I'm sure your old team wouldn't put you up for something they didn't think you could pull off."

I flash him the biggest, most genuine smile I can possibly force onto my face. "I'm good. Thinking strategy."

Walker lets out a short burst of laughter. "Wow. They were right about you. You don't waste a second, do you?"

Then he's out the door, calling back over his shoulder: "I'm going to go find your new assistant. You two should meet before your client shows up."

The next two hours pass by in a blur. I meet my new assistant, Adam, who will handle such tasks as calling for my car to be brought around and ordering my lunch.

"My car?" I say as Adam stands in front of my desk next to Walker, who is still rattling off a seemingly endless stream of information about both my job and Pierce Industries. I get it. Time is short. Christian is going to be here any minute, and I steel myself. There's no time for anything less than flawless professional behavior.

"You have company car privileges. Any time you need, you're welcome to call down to the fleet. You're welcome to take public transportation if you'd like, but a car is always available to you."

I don't have time to weigh the comfort of a company car against the extra time it will take to navigate through New

York City traffic. "Excellent. Is there anything else I should know before this meeting?" I glance at the clock on my computer screen.

We have five minutes.

"I don't think so," Walker says. "Everything you need to get started should be in the portfolio. Don't get too hung up on this meeting, though. It's mainly to feel things out. We've got other meetings already scheduled."

"Great," I say with a smile. "Thanks for everything, Walker. When I'm finished, do I report back to you?"

"Indeed," he replies. "Consider me your direct line to executive management."

With that, he turns and heads out the door, Adam following closely behind him.

"If you need anything," Adam says as he pauses in the doorway, "I'll be at my desk, right outside."

"Thanks, Adam," I say, then turn my attention back to the portfolio. I need something, anything, about Pierce Industries that I can use to keep the conversation above board. I cannot mention his eyes. I cannot mention the dreams. I cannot mention how it felt to look at him across that table all evening...

There's a light knock on the doorframe, and I look up expecting to see Adam or Walker, back with a last-minute addition to the portfolio.

Instead, I'm looking directly into Christian's eyes.

12

CHRISTIAN

"No way," I say quietly, under my breath. "No *way*."

I'm dumbfounded.

Because standing behind the desk in a swanky corner office, waiting for me, is Quinn Campbell.

In the next instant, I register the heat coming off of her, the intensity with which she's practically trembling, even though we're here for a business meeting and nothing else, professional topics only. Her eyes are locked on mine, but I can see from here that her breathing is shallow, the cut of her jacket not disguising the rise and fall of her perfect, gorgeous breasts.

I want to give myself a stern shake for being such an idiot. How could I not have gotten the name of the person I'd be meeting with? Maybe if I'd done *my* homework, I wouldn't be standing here with a racing heart and a cock so hard that it's painfully pressing against the fabric of my pants.

Jesus, she looks so *good*. The clothes she's wearing fit her so well that it's like they were custom-made for her. The pencil skirt hugs her tight, lifted ass in a way that would be obscene if it wasn't business casual.

But as much as her body is drawing me in, it's not her curves that have me captivated. It's the energy she's radiating. The pure confidence with an undercurrent of something I can't define, but it reverberates through every cell in my body.

We stand facing each other for what seems like it must be the longest moment in history, and then she leaps into action. A practiced smile spreads across her face, and she moves toward me across the office with measured steps, her hand extended.

"I don't believe we've been formally introduced," she says in an even tone. "I'm Quinn Campbell, and we'll be working together to make some strategic adjustments to your public reputation."

I take her hand and a jolt of hot lust spikes all the way up my arm, across my shoulders, and down my spine, followed quickly by the most intense need for another human being I've ever felt in my life. It's not limited to lust, or sex. I need to *know* her. Everything about her. As quickly as possible.

"Christian Pierce," I say with my signature cocky smile, shaking her hand.

I resolve right then to act like an adult. Despite our obvious and overwhelming attraction to one another, I'm not going to act on it. I'm going to keep this professional. She is a public relations expert who my father has retained on behalf of Pierce Industries. I'm one of Pierce Industries' greatest assets. This is going to be no problem.

Only I don't want to let go of her hand.

That could be a problem.

It's petite and soft in mine, and even though the handshake is well over, her hand rests in mine, holding on gently as if to feel my skin.

My charming instincts take over, and I turn her hand in mine so that the back of it is facing up, and then I bring it to my lips, a half smile on my face. "It's a pleasure to meet you," I say, kissing the back of her hand like some French troubadour.

No. Not the most professional thing to do, but it's right in line with Christian Pierce's usual playbook.

She blushes a deep red, then pulls her hand back as if I've given her an electric shock. "I've been giving some thought to a few strategies we could..." When she begins speaking, her voice is strong and clear, but I can't look away from her. Her eyes don't leave mine. They *can't* leave mine. Instead, they bore deeper into my soul, searching, *searching*.

The breath catches in my throat. I'm trying so hard, *so* hard, not to step closer to her, to take her face in my hands, to put my mouth on hers...

She bites her lip. She actually bites her bottom lip. Her lipstick is the perfect shade for her skin, and her teeth stand out white against it. She bites her lip and she takes a smooth breath that hitches at the end of the inhale, and I can't take it anymore.

I step backward and turn, then reach out and tug at the door so it releases from its magnetic doorstop. With exaggerated patience, I lay my hands flat against the surface and press it closed until finally I hear the latch catch in the lock.

It takes me one second to scan around the door. The windows that surround it are indoor glass, completely opaque.

Then I spin on my heel and I go to her. I close the distance between us in three steps and I'm on her, so close to her that the fabric of my jacket brushes against hers, and I do what I've wanted to do since I saw her in the rain last week: I put my hands on either side of her jawline and pull her toward me, covering her mouth with mine, kissing her so hard and hot and deep that the rest of the world disappears entirely.

Quinn meets every movement I make with her own, her tongue dueling with mine. Her hands go to my wrists and she pulls down like she wants to pull both of us to the floor right here, right now, but instead she compromises and lifts up onto her toes so she can get more from this kiss, more of me.

A soft moan escapes her lips and I swallow it, moving one hand down and back so that I'm cupping her head, drawing her in, never wanting this kiss to end, never wanting her to be any farther from me than she is right now.

In fact, I want her to be closer.

So much closer.

She's like no other woman on earth. She doesn't get smaller, more passive in my arms; she presses against me, she has her way with me, she's a force to be reckoned with.

I need her in my bed. I want to bend her over, give her a

little taste of the power I could have over her, and then set her free again. The city might never recover from the fireworks.

The kiss gets hotter, sloppier, her hands are gripping my wrists tighter. I'm going to lose control. I'm going to lose control and bend this woman over the desk and fuck her until—

The landline on her desk rings, the trill of it startling Quinn so that she jumps backward, her face flushed, her lips parted and puffy from the intensity of the kiss, and in two steps she's at her desk, fumbling with the phone.

"Quinn Campbell," she says into the receiver, and then she gives me a sexy little smile. "Thank you. You can send it up now." She hangs up the phone carefully. "That was my assistant—lunch has arrived."

As discreetly as I can, I adjust my rock-hard cock through my pants and step over to her desk, sitting down in one of the seats. Something is beginning to dawn on me through the steam filling my brain from how hot that kiss was. This furniture is brand new. The chairs look like they've never been touched. The suitcase in the rain...it all falls into place.

I'd bet anything this is Quinn Campbell's first day.

This makes things a hell of a lot more complicated.

Pink blush flushes her cheeks and her eyes sparkle. Cute. A professional tone, but she's struggling not to kiss me a second time.

"Well," I say, smiling at her like the cocky bastard I am. "Looks like we'll be spending some time together."

Quinn doesn't speak.

She smiles.

13

QUINN

I'm sitting across the desk from him, trying to eat the sandwich and salad that's been sent up to us as naturally as possible. I'm doing my best to act like nothing happened between us and as if there isn't this undeniably intense heat sizzling between us. My skin feels sunburned even with the office lights turned low. It takes every ounce of self-forced willpower not to let my hand visibly tremble as I lift each forkful of salad to my mouth.

Holy. *Shit.*

That was the hottest kiss I ever experienced, bar *none.* A tiny voice in the back of my mind whispers that *it's not appropriate*, that *I should* never *have kissed a client*, that *the timing is terrible,* not to mention a million other reasons why I should stand up right now, march right over to Walker's office, and tell him I'm not right for this position. Good God, my job—my *job!*—is on the line, and if anyone was to find out, if anyone was to *see...*

As loudly as my conscience is chastising me for the error of my ways, my entire *body* is screaming with passionate need. I need more of his touch. I need more of his lips. The space between my legs is steamy hot and soaking wet, almost begging me to strip off my clothes and have my way with him right here and now. There's a sleek, modern sofa positioned near one of the windows that looks perfect to accommodate a scorching hot, quick fuck.

Jesus. The strength in his arms, the pressure of his hands—it tells me how powerful he could be if he chose to be, how dominating he could be over my smaller form, and that thought turns me on more than anything else. He seemed to like my feistiness and that I wasn't going to automatically submit to him, but there's one thing I can't deny to myself—he's more than a match for me. He's not some shrinking pushover who would do shit like cheat on me with my best friend.

You don't know that, my inner voice interjects.

Fine. I *don't* know that. But what I do know is that our bodies collided with equal force. If I had let it go on long enough, one of us would have come out on top. I want it to be him. I want him to show me how much stronger he is than I am, and I'm no shrinking violet.

I swallow another bite of salad and it gets caught in my throat. I wash it down with a sip of ice-cold lemon water. The weight of the glass is pleasant in my hand, something to ground me even while my unbelievable desire makes it difficult to focus.

Still, I'm a professional, at the top of my game, and so I continue our conversation.

"Yes, we'll be looking into different photo opportunities." I'd like a photo opportunity with him in bed, naked, his body bare on the sheets so I could look at it as long as I pleased. "Do you have any philanthropic causes that you'd like to focus on over the next several weeks?"

Christian leans forward in his chair and finishes the last of his sandwich, not letting a single crumb fall to the carpet. His eyes stay locked on my face as he takes a sip of water, then raises one of HRM's cloth napkins to his lips. His perfect, soft lips that minutes ago were slipping and sliding against mine like he was claiming me as his personal property.

I can't say I minded.

"Yes," he says finally, his half-smile caressing his words with an undertone of pure sex. "Pierce Industries is dedicated to reaching out to the homeless, and we also have fostered partnerships with several hospitals across the city to provide support for research and enhanced patient care."

Every breath I take burns in my lungs. Being near him is like flirting with the surface of the sun.

"Wonderful. I can set up some appearances this week and next that will get the ball rolling on positive press coverage." I flip to a fresh page in the notepad I've been scribbling in while we ate. "As far as press releases go, is there any kind of dedication you'd like to make?"

"Dedication?" He leans back in his chair and I can see the outline of his cock through his pants. He's still hard.

"I've found that, for some of my clients, shifts in reputation seem more authentic if we can hint at some personal reason to take advantage of the opportunities. Maybe someone in your family who has inspired you? I've also had clients mention people they'd like to memorialize."

Christian takes in a deep, haggard breath and quickly looks away, his eyes dropping to focus at a crack in the floor. I've hit a nerve. But then his eyes are back locked on mine. There's that charged connection between us again, strong as ever.

"There are a couple of people I would—" He starts speaking in a soft tone, but then trails off. "My mother spent a lot of time on charity work before she died."

Oh, Christ. That tidbit was probably in the portfolio. I can't imagine losing my mother, even though she and my father have gone a little buck wild in their retirement years and rarely stay in the same place for more than a few weeks at a time. At least I know I can always *call* her. "I'm so sorry," I say softly.

"It's all right," he says, with that rakish smile that I know I'll never be able to get out of my head. "It's been a few years. My father won't have any problem with mentioning her in a press release."

The heaviness of the moment settles on my shoulders. I'm an idiot. I look over my notes. We've covered *more* than enough ground for this meeting. Honestly, if he stays in here any longer, I might tear off all my clothes and throw myself at him.

And that would be a disaster for us both.

I stand up from my seat and Christian follows suit. "Thank you for coming in to meet with me, Christian," I say, offering him my hand. "I'll see you on Wednesday for our next appointment."

He takes it, and a shock of desire explodes in my chest.

One tug and two steps, and he's got me around the side of the desk, inches away from him, and he leans down to whisper into my ear. The words he says make me even wetter and my heart beat harder.

"You'll see me before then. Did you think I'd ignore that kiss?"

Then he's gone, leaving me breathless and shaking in my office, my body begging for him to come back.

14

CHRISTIAN

In the elevator on the way down to the lobby of HRM's building, I put my fingers to my lips. The imprint of Quinn's kisses is still there, down where she took my lip between her teeth and *bit*, hard enough to drive me insanely wild.

I sensed it the moment I saw her, but that kiss—that epic collision of a kiss—has confirmed it for me. She's like no one I've ever met.

Then watching her sit through the rest of that meeting, so cool, so collected...

At least on the outside.

I saw how her breath caught in her throat. I saw the flushed color in her cheeks, the way she darted her tongue out to lick her bottom lip.

She wanted more of me as badly as I wanted more of her.

If it were anyone else, I might have taken the risk.

I might have bent her over on all fours on that little sofa in her office and fucked her until she clenched and spasmed in an orgasm around my cock, her coral dress shoved up around her waist to allow me access.

If it was anyone else, I wouldn't care quite so much about screwing up her job for her. I wouldn't care so much about adding yet another notch to my playboy belt. Christian Pierce can't help himself. He takes what he wants, and then he discards the leftovers. That's the game.

But not with her.

No, with her it's different. This is so much more powerful. I'm swept away, and I'm the one who initiated the kiss.

It's different—yet I'm fooling myself. I *did* take a risk like that. It might be an even bigger gamble than taking her from behind in her new office.

Shit. What the hell was I *thinking* when I told her I'd see her again before Wednesday?

There—right *there*. That was the biggest risk of all.

I've set myself up.

In so many ways.

I want to see her. I *need* to see her. I need it more than I've ever needed anything in my entire life, and it's more than the insane attraction to her gorgeous body. Knowing more about her is an itch I have to scratch, and secondhand information won't be enough. It would also be weird to ask Carolyn the kinds of questions I want to ask Quinn.

There's the added complication that she's been assigned to handle my PR. As far as I can see, there's not a good way to get around that. My father hand-selected the firm. I don't know his reasons, and I don't need to, but switching firms isn't an option. I doubt he'd accept my reasoning, which is essentially that I need to date the woman who's handling Pierce Industries—me—as a client.

Another twist: I can't appear to be hung up on her. I can't appear to always have her on my mind. I can't appear to be losing sleep because I can't get thoughts of her smile, her voice, her curves out of my mind. That kiss. That *kiss*. My cock twitches thinking about the heat of her mouth on mine, and how if we'd been the only two people in the building, I would have dragged my mouth down the side of her neck, torn off her blazer and that little coral dress underneath, spread her legs, and...

And lost myself entirely.

That's what I can't do.

That's what I can't do under any circumstances, even for a woman like Quinn Campbell. Even though the world shifted underneath my feet when we kissed. Even though she responded to me like she was born to kiss me, born to touch me, born to fuck me.

I can't treat her any differently than all the other women. Three dates maximum.

I laugh out loud. Three dates? How am I supposed to take Quinn on three dates when *she works for me*? That'll be a red flag. If we're going to see each other at all, it's going to be in secret.

She must know that. She must know sleeping with a client is a surefire way to lose her job.

Of course she knows. She's excellent at what she does. That's why they assigned her to me, New York City's most notorious playboy.

Yet she didn't say no. She didn't draw back. She didn't fight it.

She pressed into me. She wanted *more.*

There's a thought in the back of my mind that's like the third rail. I don't want to touch it, but as I exit HRM's building and climb into the back of the Town Car, it becomes impossible to avoid.

The secret.

My secret.

That's the real, true risk in all of this. There would be a way to find another PR firm, another, lesser version of Quinn Campbell to arrange media appearances and smooth out my reputation so that Pierce Industries isn't ashamed of me.

But they would be—everyone would be—if they knew the truth.

Deep down, I know that if I let Quinn get too close, if I let her break all my rules, break down all my walls, she'll eventually come to know everything about me.

Everything.

Once she knows everything there is to know about Christian Pierce, she'll leave, and she'll never look back.

"Back to the office?" Louis says from the front of the Town Car.

"That's right," I tell him. As he pulls the car away from the curb, I close my eyes and let myself go back to that kiss. To the taste of her that still lingers on my lips.

This is not going to end well. I know it in my bones.

But I can't turn away from this inferno of passion.

I'm going to get burned.

15

QUINN

Monday night is sheer agony. I follow my regular routine—I go home to the apartment like nothing is wrong, change out of my coral dress and blazer and pull on the same stretchy yoga pants and tank top that I traveled here in, and then plant myself on Carolyn's couch.

I'm still reeling from the aftershocks of Christian's kiss like crackling electrical charges through my hands, my feet, my legs. I catch myself raising my fingertips to my slightly swollen lips. It felt so good to be pressed up against him, to let those carnal urges flash boldly and run wild through my body...

I'm about to flee back into my bedroom to relieve some of the almost unbearable sexual pressure on my own when Carolyn breezes through the front door. She hangs up her purse on one of the hooks in the entryway with a flourish. "Hey, Q!" she says, and I sit up straight.

"Good day at work?" I ask.

"*Great* day." She waltzes into the living room with a spring in her step and surveys my outfit. She raises her eyebrows in question. "I see you're in for the evening. I take it your day *wasn't* great?"

I can't help smiling, because that kiss—oh, my God, that kiss—would have outweighed even the worst day. It was paralyzingly good.

"No way. It was good for my first day at headquarters." I want to tell someone what happened between Christian and me, but I hesitate. Carolyn knows him. He won't want this shared freely among his circle of friends. "The office is..." I search for the words even as I give her a huge grin. "High energy."

"That's awesome!" she says, relief spreading visibly across her face. "I hate to say this, but I—I kind of forgot it was your first day. It seems like you've been here forever."

I laugh out loud. "Is that a good thing?"

"*Yes*," my roommate answers sincerely. "Jess would approve."

She crosses into the kitchen and I hear her open and close a drawer, then I hear her pop a cork from a bottle of wine. She reemerges a minute later with two stemless wine glasses. She kicks off her black high-heeled shoes, and joins me on the couch, letting out a happy sigh as she hands me a drink.

"Cheers!" Carolyn says brightly, before we clink the glasses together, then take a celebratory sip.

"Tell me about your day," I say once she's leaned back against the cushions. "What was so great about it?"

"I quit my job!"

My jaw drops. Carolyn has a trust fund—she'll never want for money—but this seems like a drastic lifestyle change. "*What*?"

She waves her hand dismissively in the air. "No, no, it's not what you think. I've been planning this for a while, but with Jess moving out and you moving in...What's happening is —" Carolyn leans in like she's telling me a secret, her eyes sparkling. "I'm opening a clothing boutique two blocks west of here. It's going to be eclectic—fashion pieces I'm going to source from all over the country, plus some of my own artistic pieces. I've got the startup money, and if it goes under—not that it's going to—but if it goes under, I can always go back to media production."

"That's amazing, Care!" I say, and as the words leave my mouth, I'm overwhelmed by how much I want to tell her about Christian. But I can't. "Wine isn't enough! We need food. *Lots* of food."

"Are you thinking what I'm thinking?" Carolyn can't stop smiling about her newest venture.

"*Chinese*!" we both say in unison, and break down in giggles.

Once we've finished up the sweet and sour chicken and egg rolls and the credits have run for the final movie, my lust for Christian starts creeping back in, slowly ramping up throughout the evening until my entire body throbs. By the time Carolyn says goodnight, I'm coiled tight around my desire. We move through the apartment, turning off all the lights, checking to make sure the door is locked, and then I make a mad dash to my bedroom.

After hastily brushing my teeth, I strip off the yoga pants and slide under the covers wearing my panties and tank top.

I want him so badly.

I could text him right now.

That's the worst part.

I have his cell number in case I need to contact him outside of business hours for a PR emergency.

This is an emergency, but it doesn't have to do with his reputation...at least not yet.

Instead, I slip my hand down across the smooth skin of my stomach, down, *down* underneath the silky fabric of my panties until my fingers make contact with my aching clit. Then, while imagining Christian's hard masculine body pressed against me, I get myself off—once, then twice, before I fall asleep.

~

I'm wishing I could spend most of the day somewhere private. It doesn't help that Christian is my one and only client, so all my working hours are dedicated to him. Looking at his picture. Piecing together a tentative schedule of social appearances designed to smooth out the rough edges of his reputation to convince the public that that he's mature and professional enough to run a Fortune 500 company.

My attention *is* focused on Christian, but I can't concentrate on what I'm *supposed* to be doing, only the hot, steady pulsing between my legs, begging for a release that can't be satisfied in the office.

Christian could help me with that, though, the voice in my head taunts me.

"Ha." I let out a short burst of laughter under my breath. Christian Pierce could give me what I needed at any time and in virtually any location. I'm positive about that.

He said he would see me before our meeting tomorrow. That meeting is at ten o'clock.

As the hours crawl by, the possibility of seeing him today becomes completely distracting. I want to do nothing but lean back in my chair and imagine all the things we could do together—all the things that *he* could do to *me*—but through sheer willpower, I force myself to doggedly keep building the schedule of appearances, keep writing sample press releases, keep my phone tucked into my purse.

If he wants to see me, he'll call.

There's always the chance that he didn't mean what he said. I've met plenty of rich, arrogant guys who go back on their word or make promises with no intention of keeping them. I've been engaged to one such asshole who never meant what he said, so it wouldn't be the first time that I've fallen for someone like that.

I'm wound so tight that by the time five o'clock rolls around and the office empties out, I can't bring myself to leave. I stare at my computer screen, finishing tasks that could very easily be left for tomorrow, until it's nearly six o'clock.

He still hasn't called or sent a message of any kind.

My heart sinks as I ride the elevator down to the lobby alone. Unless he's planning some early-morning rendezvous —and how could he do that without letting Carolyn in on it?—then his word was a playful half-promise, not to be trusted.

My disappointment shocks me.

Until I see the Town Car pulled up to the curb, the driver leaning against it.

He straightens to his full height when he sees me coming. "Ms. Campbell?"

"Yes, that's me," I answer, my heart starting to beat heavily. Whose car is this? I didn't order a ride home. Should I be ready to run in case this is some kind of bizarre kidnapping attempt?

"Mr. Pierce sent me to pick you up. He'd like to meet with you."

I bite my lip, hesitating. This is so wrong. It's such a risk. I should leave right now and put an end to this whole thing.

"Can I see your I.D.?" I say, buying myself a little more time.

The man produces an I.D. wallet and shows it to me, smiling so that his expression matches the photo on his license. His name is Louis.

"How do I know you work for Mr. Pierce?"

He pulls a cell phone from his jacket pocket and presses a single button. Waits for one second. Christian's voice sounds from the other end of the line. "Pierce," he says.

"Ms. Campbell would like to make sure I work for you." Then he hands me the phone.

"Hello?" I say, trying to keep my cool.

"It's me," Christian says, and the sound of his voice makes my insides melt. "Come to me. Right now."

I hang up the call.

I can still walk away.

This could all be over.

But I don't.

I give Louis a single nod, and he reaches across in front of me and pulls open the door of the Town Car. I scramble into the back seat, and he closes the door behind me.

Here goes nothing.

16

CHRISTIAN

Even after the phone call, I'm still not entirely certain that she's going to show. Louis sent me a message saying that they were en route, but it's not like he's going to flip her over his shoulder and haul her up here if she changes her mind. This entire thing is taking much longer than I thought it would. I'd figured Quinn for the type who would leave the office right at five, and instead Louis lingered out by the curb for a full hour before she showed.

A full hour of me, pacing this apartment, my heart pounding like it's banging on the door of my chest.

I take another lap around my space on the Upper East Side. It's significantly smaller than my penthouse in Midtown, but it serves its purpose: having a place to entertain women that reveals nothing whatsoever about the real me.

I chose all the furniture, of course. Well, I chose the designer who chose the furniture according to my specifications. I have the place cleaned once a week, but it's more like a hotel suite than a truly lived-in space.

I have plenty of personal things here. The closets are stocked with my clothes, and the bathroom has a full complement of towels embroidered with my initials. The design still looks strange, after all this time, but the towels are plush as hell and the cleaning woman arranges them perfectly every time she's here.

There's nothing *truly* personal.

There are no family photos and only a few token books. For a while, back in high school, I kept a journal—who the hell knows why—but I've long since broken myself of the habit of writing down any kind of detailed accounting of my life.

It's too risky.

Jesus Christ, how long does it *take* to drive here?

I'm desperate to see her, even though the smallest part of me hopes she won't arrive.

If Quinn sidesteps this like a true professional, if she puts that insane, hot connection between us second to her work priorities, it will make my life significantly easier in the long run.

Would it?

The pesky devil's advocate taunting me from the back of my mind can't shut his mouth. I don't know. That's the bitch of it. I don't know if it would be easier, in the long run, to live without someone like Quinn.

That's a cop-out. *To live without Quinn.*

There's something about this woman that I can't shake. I can't go on without fully exploring her and learning everything there is to know about her. Who knows—maybe we're a total mismatch, but the way her body felt against mine, the way her mouth opened to let my tongue have its way with hers, the way she kissed me back—it all tells me that we're perfectly matched, we're so compatible that it would be an utter waste to stay away from each other.

It's like lighting a match near gasoline. One of us is going to go up in flames, and I have no doubt that person is going to be me.

I can never tell her.

What would Quinn even say if she knew? If she knew the truth about me?

I am one hundred percent certain that she would react coolly to finding out that—

I shake my head, ending it there. I can't go there. I can't. It's been too long. *Nobody* would take that kind of news in stride, much less someone who was in love with me.

Oh, my God. She's not in love with me. We're not in love.

Aren't you?

I flop down on the sofa, putting a hand to my forehead.

I can't deny there's a current of something running wild and deep and true between us, but what does that mean for the future? There are no guarantees. Not ever.

I'm restless. I sit down and get back up again to look through the window at the street below.

Out of the line of traffic, I see a black Town Car disengage from the main flow of traffic and head for the curb.

Spinning on my heel, I turn away from the window. I don't want to see if she's standing me up.

Taking in a deep breath, I try to force myself to be calm, cool, collected. *The truth is*, I remind myself sternly, *this, right now, is about the fact that the two of you need to have your hands on one another. There's no point in speculating about what that means. There's no point in getting hung up on the possibility of a relationship you can never have. You are still in control.*

I'm in control.

There's a soft knock at the front door of my apartment. My heart pounds, control or not.

I make my way to the door with slow, measured steps. I won't give myself away by rushing to open it.

The doorknob is cool and smooth under my hand as I twist it, pulling the heavy door open.

She came.

Quinn stands in the hallway wearing an all-black ensemble that emphasizes the lithe lines of her waist and hips. Her dark hair is pulled back into a gleaming twist at the back of her head.

She looks gorgeous.

Her breath is already coming hard in her chest, and for a long moment we both stand there, staring into each other's eyes. There's pink color rising in her cheeks, coloring her creamy skin with a delicate blush.

The moment shatters, breaks, and then the pieces spin back together.

I reach for her hand.

I pull her inside.

I close the door behind her.

Then she's on me like an animal, arms flung around my neck, grasping, her mouth crashing against my mouth, her teeth biting at my lip. Her shoes fall from her feet and onto the floor as I lift her up in my arms. She wraps her lithe legs tightly around my waist, and I flex my muscles, bringing her in closer even as I taste her so deeply that it makes the kiss we shared in the office seem like a peck on the cheek.

I'm drowning in her.

I love it.

I'm so fucked.

17

QUINN

I am silent on the ride from Midtown to the Upper East Side, but my mind buzzes and hums with thoughts of him. My lips still burn with yesterday's kiss. The space between my legs has been soaked with my desire since he left me.

He could be my downfall, but my body can't resist him.

The moment I got into the car, it was all over.

Once the decision was made, my mind went into a kind of sexual overdrive, and as Louis steers the car through the New York City traffic, I look out the window but see nothing. Not the buildings, not the people hustling by, not an ounce of the life that teems here in the concrete jungle. I am consumed with imagining Christian and his touch, his kiss, his body.

Maybe he's already dismissed what happened earlier and intends to show me, right now, that it was a one-time mistake that won't be repeated. Maybe he's going to sit me down across from a desk in one of his private buildings somewhere and ask me to discuss the plans I've come up with to enhance his image. Maybe that's how he works—he draws you in and then, when he has you where he wants you, hook, line, and sinker, he lets you dangle before cutting the rope and watching you fall.

I shake my head, my lips pressed together. No. This can't be related to the work I do for him in the office. I felt the passion in our kiss. I felt the mutual need, so hot it almost scorched the walls of my office.

He's summoning me because he can't bear to be away from me one second longer.

I know how he feels.

I *don't* know what it is about him that's making me so crazy, so willing to disregard my commitment to professionalism and sneak away to do God knows what with one of my clients on the second day at my new job. And it can't be that his body makes my mouth water even when it's hidden under tailored suits, not an inch of skin showing. It's more than that, but what? Is it the look in his eyes when he talks to me? Is it the electricity that charges through our veins when we both touch? Is it something deeper, wilder?

The car comes to a stop, parking curbside somewhere north of Midtown.

We're here.

~

Louis gives me a key card. "Use this to access the elevator inside. The doorman is expecting you. Top floor." Then he turns and gets back into the Town Car without another word.

I take a deep breath, force myself to stand up straight, and lift my chin in an attempt to gather a burst of confidence before moving inside the building.

He wants me to be here, and I want to be here. The only thing left to do is let this scene play out.

I stride confidently into the lobby of the building, It's fairly nondescript, although there are small touches of luxury everywhere I look—marble flooring and countertops in the lobby, a uniformed doorman who gives me a wink and a smile as I go past, my heels echoing with every step, whisper-quiet elevators. The air inside is cool and comfortable, a welcome break from the summer heat.

The elevator doors slide open as soon as I wave the card in front of one of the scanners embedded in the wall. Blessedly, the car is empty, so I'm left in peace to push the button for the eighth floor. The penthouse.

Moments later, the elevator deposits me in a silent plushly carpeted hallway. Five steps away from the elevator, a single door is set into an alcove in the wall.

If I lose my nerve now, I'll never go in. I step up to the door and rap on it lightly with my knuckles.

Then I wait.

It seems to take forever before the door opens, the moments dripping languidly down the chain of time as if my heart is not pounding, as if my mouth is not suddenly dry.

The door swings inward.

There he is.

I look into his crystalline blue eyes for one long moment. Finally, he extends his hand to grasp mine, and he pulls me inside the entryway, closing the door behind us. He turns to face me.

I cannot remain silent and still.

My need, my overflowing lust boils over.

No, I cannot remain silent and still another second.

I throw myself at him. As soon as our bodies connect I wrap my arms around his neck. Our lips lock together like we're on a plane plummeting toward the ocean and have only moments left to live, and I plunge my tongue deeply into his mouth, I bite at his lip. He responds to me in kind like he can't control his animalistic urge. Without realizing it, I wrap both my legs around his waist, hiking my skirt up around my hips. His arms flex against me, pressing me even tighter into his hard body. We fit together. Perfectly.

He lets out a low groan and puts one hand to the back of my head, taking control of the kiss, forcing his tongue into my mouth to taste and devour, and then he's moving us, still hooked together, through the apartment. Moments later, we're in his bedroom. He tips us both onto the bed, crawling on and over me, his arms on either side of me as he dives in for another kiss that draws a whimper from me.

I need him and he knows it.

He leaps off the bed and strips off his clothes. I can't help but gasp at the perfection that is Christian Pierce in the nude—ripped abs, muscular arms, and a cock so thick and long, already hard and pulsing, that for the briefest moment, I wonder if it will fit inside. He's beautiful.

Then he's back on the bed, kissing me hard and tearing at my clothes. Soon they're tossed in a pile on the floor next to his, and I'm splayed out before him, my arms and legs thrown wide.

My mind is empty except for one word. "Please."

It rings like a bell in the silence between us, and a half-smile that lights me aflame spreads across Christian's face.

He leans down over me, balancing himself above me on his elbows, and nips at my earlobe. "Please what?"

"Please, you have to fuck me."

"I *have* to fuck you?" His voice is quiet and deep and every word out of his mouth creates an inferno in me that can only be quenched by one thing.

I turn and look him directly in the eye. "I *know* you do."

"Hmmm," he says, leaning to the side, tracing one finger down the side of my neck, over my collarbone, and down to my nipple, which he circles as if he has all the time in the world, and then he rolls it between his fingers. I moan softly at the spikes of pleasure shooting straight down my spine to my aching wet pussy. "You might be right about that."

"I *am* right about that," I pant.

He plants kisses on the side of my neck, his hot breath brushing against my skin. "You have quite the attitude, Quinn Campbell. I wonder if I can tame it."

My hips roll and writhe underneath him as my desperation

grows, and at the words “tame it” a new gush of wetness soaks the inside of my thighs. Yes. *Yes*. I want to be tamed by him, taken by him, claimed as his.

“There’s only one way to find out,” I say, trying my hardest to raise my hips up to make contact.

Something in my voice gets under his skin, strips him of his remaining self-control, and the next instant his hand is under my jaw, gripping my neck with a gentle force as he covers my mouth with his, our lips crushed together. With the other hand he spreads me wider, then positions the head of his cock at my slick opening.

Then, with his free hand—Jesus, how does he know the secret fantasies I’ve never told anyone?—he catches both of my hands and pins them above my head.

“You don’t know it,” he says, flicking his tongue against my jawline, “but you’re already mine.”

Then he slams his hardness into me, filling me to the hilt, sending me crashing down in an explosion of pleasure that goes on and on and on.

18

CHRISTIAN

Quinn is insatiable, wild, begging for me to bring her under control even as she sasses me, fights me, tries to drive me crazy.

It works.

I fuck her hard and fast, and she spreads herself open for me, taking every last inch of my cock, crying out, moaning. She cannot get enough of me.

The feeling is mutual.

We're not finished after the first round. She spends ten minutes with her head buried in my shoulder and then her hips rock against mine once again.

She wants *more*.

I'm not going to deny her what she wants.

I want it, too. I need it.

With one movement, I have her on her hands and knees and I'm inside her again, moving slowly this time, every stroke powerful. Her body shudders underneath me as she waits for me to plow all the way inside. As I pull back, her pussy clenches around my cock, trying to keep me buried deep inside, and it's so intense that the edges of my vision go black.

When we've finished this round, she collapses onto her belly on the bed, murmuring something incoherent, the tone sexy and satisfied, and I curl up around her, the little quivering aftershocks pulsing through her body.

We lay in silence for about twenty minutes, and then she stirs, rolls over, propping up her head on her arm. She looks pink and flushed, and there's a look in her eyes that I can't quite identify.

"So, Christian Pierce," she says, idly tracing her fingertips over one of my shoulders and down my arm. "Do you think we should discuss what happened?"

"What is there to discuss?" I say with a grin. We both know this won't be the only time. A flash of cold fear goes through me. *What if this* is *the only time?* A warm buzz overtakes the fear, washing it away.

She rolls her eyes with a smile. "You're one of my clients," she says matter-of-factly.

"What's the problem with that?"

"I could get fired, for one."

"You won't get fired."

"If anyone at HRM finds out about this, I will."

I lean in and kiss her gently, then suck at her bottom lip. "They won't find out."

She takes in a sharp breath. She's dying to trust me, but if my hunch is correct, Quinn Campbell isn't the kind of her girl to take any asshole at his word.

"They won't find out if we end this right now." Her words come out as a whisper, and though she tries to keep her voice neutral, I can hear how much she wants me to disagree with her.

So I do.

"We can't end this right now." Someday. Not now.

"We should."

"What we should do is..." I let the pause hang in the air while I run the flat of my hand over the curve of her waist. "Shower. And then have dinner together."

Her eyes sparkling, Quinn's smile gets even wider. "Are you asking me out on a *date*?"

I pretend to scoff. "Why do you think I invited you here?"

"For sex, obviously."

"That, too."

We both laugh, and then a look of concern crosses her face. "I don't have anything with me to wear on a date."

"Don't worry," I say, climbing off the bed and offering her my hand. "I meant dinner *in*." She stands up and I give myself several moments to marvel at the utter perfection of her naked body—the slim waist, the full breasts, the way her shoulders curve so delicately to meet her neck. "The bathroom is that way." I point towards the master bath located off my bedroom. "You hop into the shower, and I'll have the food sent up."

Quinn puts a hand on either side of my face and draws me down for a kiss. "Will I be seeing you in the shower?"

"I wouldn't miss it."

~

Twenty minutes later, she's sitting at my dining table wearing one of the plush robes from my bathroom. Like my towels, the robe also bears my initials embroidered onto the front pocket. I like the look of it on her. Like I've made my mark in more ways than one.

You know this is going to be a disaster.

I know it.

But I'm still on the first date.

And right now it seems like heaven.

Quinn is glowing, her hair wet from the shower and combed away from her face, and she takes evident delight in every single forkful of the dinner I've had sent over from a five-star restaurant called Moods.

"This is incredible," she says, lifting another tender morsel of some kind of extravagantly prepared chicken—I didn't ask, I trusted that my celebrity chef friend could handle the menu—between her lips. "I didn't even know you could get delivery from a place like that."

I let out a laugh. "You can get *takeout* from anywhere if you have enough money and send a driver to pick it up. They did deliver this, however. I own part of the restaurant."

"Of *course* you do." Her eyes shine with pleasure, but she doesn't seem to be intensely focused on my billions.

It's refreshing.

Once I break out the wine, the conversation begins to flow.

"What made you move to New York? And *stay*, after the welcome you got?" I ask several minutes later as Quinn devours chocolate blackout cake.

She shakes her head, the glimpse of sadness first rushing over her face disappearing into a look of resignation. "I wish I could tell you that I wanted to come here, but I hate when people lie about stupid shit." Quinn looks me directly in the eye. "My fiancé cheated on me. With my best friend. So I asked for a transfer."

"Oh, shit. I'm sorry," I say, reaching across the table for her hand.

She takes another sip of wine. "It was pretty unbelievable. After that, I didn't want to stay in my house. I didn't want to stay in Colorado. I'm lucky Carolyn wanted a roommate."

"I think she misses Jess more than she lets on."

"I can imagine! That massive apartment must be lonely with only one person rattling around."

I think of my own penthouse in Midtown, the rooms filled with my things. None of it matters.

It's going to be hard to end things with Quinn. The scene isn't going to be pretty.

I get lost in thought for a moment too long.

Quinn fills in the silence.

"You didn't tell me you had a tattoo," she comments casually, and my heart stops.

I hardly ever think about it. It almost never comes up, since I usually bring women here in the dead of night, in the dark, and I'm dressed before they're out of bed. A frigid anxiety twists my gut.

When I look across at Quinn, her eyes are filled with concern. "Are you okay?"

"Yeah," I say, too quickly. "Yeah, it's nothing." I laugh and the tone of it convinces her. "My mind wandered for a second there." Then I give her a devilish stare. "Maybe we should go back to bed."

Quinn's face slowly relaxes, and then she smiles. "Race you."

19

QUINN

Carolyn is sitting on the couch in the living room when I get back, even though it's almost midnight. She has several binders spread out on the table in front of her and a pencil tucked behind her ear. When I step through the door, she starts in on me in a panicked voice.

"Quinn!" she cries, then grabs up her phone from the table. "Oh, my God, it's late." She gives her head a little shake as if to clear some cobwebs, then gives me a second look. "Wait. Have you been at work?"

"No," I say, laughing. "But it looks like *you* have. Is this stuff for the boutique?"

"Yeah," Carolyn says with a little sigh. "I left some details to finalize after I was done with the other job, but it turns out there's more to do than I thought."

"Shit." I drop down onto the couch next to her. "When are you planning to open?"

"Next Friday."

"You've got time, then," I say lightly.

"Not much time." She blows her breath out through her lips. "I mean, the store is mostly set up, but I still have things to go through and—" She waves a hand at the binders. "You know."

I nod sagely, though I wouldn't know the first thing about running a boutique. All I know is how to shop in them.

Carolyn laughs. "It's good to know I have your support."

"You totally do."

She narrows her eyes. "If you weren't at work, where were you? I'm dying to know." Then she puts a hand over her mouth. "It's none of my business."

I need to share this—at least part of it—with a friend. My former best friend isn't an option, and I don't have a sister. Carolyn is the closest person to me.

I can trust her.

"Swear you won't say a word about it." I look her straight in the eye.

Her face instantly lights up. Everyone loves gossip, and it's a pretty safe bet that Carolyn, like anyone else, loves secrets. "I won't," she says solemnly.

"I'm serious, Care."

"I'm serious, too."

I take a deep breath and let it out slowly. "Maybe we should have some wine." I only had a single glass at Christian's.

"It's midnight!"

"It's the perfect time." I leap up from the couch and cross into the kitchen while Carolyn tucks some stray papers back into her binders. When I come back with two glasses of white wine, she's tucked her legs underneath her and is leaned back into the arm of the couch.

"Don't keep me in suspense, Q. It's not fair."

"Okay," I say, settling in and pulling a blanket over my legs. "I was at Christian Pierce's apartment."

Carolyn's eyes go wide, and the wine glass freezes halfway to her lips. "*What*?"

"I don't know—" I break off, searching for a way to make this seem less crazy than it probably is. "The other night when he helped me with my luggage, there was something...between us, you know? And then we ran into him at the Swan, and then—Care, you're never going to believe this. He's my client at HRM."

"Your *client*?"

"Literally, he's my *only* client. That promotion I told you about?"

Carolyn nods and sips quickly at her wine. It's like she doesn't want to have any in her mouth to spit out at my next outrageous statement.

"They assigned me to the Pierce account. And my only project for the foreseeable future is enhancing Christian's image."

"Oh, my God," she says quietly. "How did *that* end up with you at his apartment?"

"We had our first meeting yesterday. And he kissed me."

Carolyn laughs out loud, the sound petering out into a giggle in the end. "That guy cannot keep his dick in his pants. Is that why he needs PR services?"

"I'd imagine." I can't stop myself from blushing. "He got promoted at Pierce Industries, so..."

She takes one look at my face, and her mouth drops open. "Why is your face so *red*? Did you *sleep* with him?" Her voice is rising in pitch. Before the end of this conversation it's going to sound like she inhaled the helium from a balloon.

"Yes!" I cry, covering my face with my free hand.

"Quinn!" Carolyn admonishes, then dissolves into laughter. "It was a one-time fling, right? I mean, he's hot—I'll be the first to admit it."

"I don't know if it's a fling or not."

I look back into her eyes, and her expression gets serious.

"You could lose your job over that, right?"

"Yeah."

We're both silent for a moment, deep in thought. Then Carolyn says, "Well, was he any good?"

"Oh, my God," I groan. "He was *so* good."

We both laugh, so hard that tears come to my eyes. I brush one away as the laughter tapers off. "But seriously, Care—there's something—we have something that's—"

She holds up one hand. "Don't bother explaining yourself to

me." Her eyes are glittering with excitement. "I can't believe the two of you hooked up. No—I can believe it. The way you two were talking at the Swan…there's some serious attraction there."

"I'd say."

"Be careful, Quinn. He tends to be—"

"I know. I'm managing his *reputation*, remember?"

She nods again, a wistful look on her face

"There was one weird moment at his place, though."

Carolyn perks back up. "What was it?"

"He had arranged dinner for…*after*." My roommate covers her mouth with her hand to stifle another peal of laughter. I smile, shaking my head. "And while we were eating, I mentioned his tattoo."

There's a flash of confusion on Carolyn's face, and then her expression softens into sympathy. "And he got weird about it?"

"Yeah. He totally froze up. Tried to cover up his reaction, but it was obvious I had touched upon a sensitive subject."

She shifts position on the couch, clearing her throat. "There's a reason for that."

"*Please* share."

Carolyn considers me thoughtfully. "Did you get a file about his background when you took him on as a client?"

"I haven't read through all of it yet."

"This will probably be in there somewhere, so I guess in the end I'm not telling you anything you won't find out sooner or later." She swallows. "Christian had a twin brother."

"*Had*?"

"Had. Jess and I were best friends with the two of them in boarding school."

A sinking sense of dread fills the pit of my stomach. "What happened to him?"

"He died. Not long after they turned eighteen."

I look down into my wine glass, my heart breaking for Christian. "How?"

"I heard it was a drug overdose, but Chris almost never talks about it."

"Jesus. Is the tattoo for his brother?"

"No. Eli—his brother—had the same one. They got matching tattoos the same week that he died."

"Oh, man."

"Don't worry about it, Q. If he moved on in the conversation, it's probably fine."

I bite at my lip, then nod. "We did go back to bed after that."

Carolyn rolls her eyes with a gigantic grin. "I'd say it's more than fine."

My wine glass emptied, I stand up from the couch, suddenly bone-tired. "Thanks for telling me all that, Care. I'm going to head to bed."

"Me, too." She rises from the couch with a yawn and goes to turn out the lights.

I'm almost to my bedroom when she calls after me. "Don't think you're off the hook, though. I want updates!"

I can't wipe the stupid smile off my face. "You'll get them. Don't you worry."

20

CHRISTIAN

I have never met a more impressive woman than Quinn Campbell.

At our Wednesday meeting, she sits across her desk from me, cool and collected, as if I didn't fuck her senseless last night.

The fact that she can be so professional—*friendly*, even—in the face of overwhelming sexual tension makes me want to bend her over the desk and take her here and now, even more than I already did.

"This strategy will begin to unfold this week, if you don't have any issues with the events or the timing," she says, sliding the printed calendar of scheduled public appearances across the glass surface of her desk toward me. "The first opportunity I've arranged is on Friday at the Bowery Mission, helping to serve meals during the dinner shift. I have some press tentatively booked to be there so you can announce the donation you're making in your mother's memory."

I look up into her fiery green eyes and grin. “I’m making a donation in my mother’s memory?”

“Don’t get cute with me, Mr. Pierce,” she shoots back, the corner of her mouth quirked in a smile. It’s the first time during the meeting that the real Quinn—at least, what I assume to be the real Quinn, based on how raw and passionate she was last night—breaks through in her professional persona. “You’ll make this donation, and you’ll like doing it.”

That’s what I’m talking about. Although, on second glance, she probably has a reputation in the industry for her no-bullshit client-handling skills.

She’s a woman of many talents.

“I don’t disagree,” I answer, laughing. My heart aches a little at the thought of my mother. “Mom would be proud.”

“Yes,” she says, a softer tone in her voice. “Listen, Christian...”

This isn’t the businesslike self that she’s been presenting most of the meeting. I’m sure of it now. I lean toward her even though the door to the office is closed tightly. “What is it?”

“I read through your file this morning to get a more thorough picture of your background,” she says slowly, and at first I have no idea where this is going. So what if she read through the file? What does that have to do with—?

“I read about your brother.”

I never talk about my brother.

I try my best not to *think* of my brother.

I can't think of a single thing to say.

"I'm sorry for bringing him up," she says, straightening her posture, worry filling her eyes. "I wanted to let you know that...that I had read about him, and if there was anything you wanted to—"

A hot surge of anger spikes through my chest, and one of my hands involuntarily clenches into a fist. "No."

"I'm—"

I cut her off. "I'm not using him to boost my image."

Underneath the anger, fear rankles in my gut.

Quinn holds up both hands like I'm a bull about to tear into a matador. "That's not what I was suggesting," she says smoothly. I'm soothed by the sound of her voice in spite of myself. "I wanted to share with you that I'm aware of him, okay? I'm—" She leans in again, dropping her hands to the surface of the desk. "I can't do this. I need to be honest."

"Honest about what?" My anger is already dissipating.

She bites her lip, then looks me straight in the eye. "I told Carolyn that we...that we went on a date."

I burst out laughing. "I bet she loved that."

"She did," Quinn says in a tentative tone, a little smile forming on her face. "And I—I mentioned that I thought I hit a nerve by asking about your tattoo. She told me about Elijah, and then I saw his name again in your file."

I sigh and straighten my spine, though I want to sink back into the chair and cover my eyes with my hand. I can't let her see how much talking about this scares the shit out of me, and I'm not going to start breaking down now, after ten years. Christian Pierce isn't some shrinking sissy who falls apart at the mention of his deceased brother. "It's all right, Quinn." I force all the thoughts about Eli out of my mind and concentrate hard on the memory of Quinn's creamy skin pressed up against the length of my body, let the memory put a smile on my face. "Can I be honest about something?"

"Anything."

I stand up out of the chair and lean across to whisper into her ear. "I want to bend you over this desk and fuck you until you can't possibly orgasm even one more time."

Then I sit back in my seat and watch her.

Heat rises to Quinn's cheeks, turning her face a deep shade of red, and her lips part slightly. I can only imagine how slick her folds must be right now underneath the sharp black dress she's wearing today, the sleeveless cut showing off her toned arms. Her fingers curl into her palms as she stares into my eyes, the gold flecks in her green irises glinting in the afternoon sun pouring through her office windows. I only see the rise of her breasts because I'm looking for it. My cock twitches. It doesn't matter that my heart is still pounding from how close, how *close* she was to seeing something that could have screwed everything up permanently...

She looks down at the papers in front of her, blinks, then takes one of them into her hands.

"The second opportunity will be two weeks from next Tuesday, and this is one that I've set up to be on behalf of Pierce Industries to show your commitment there. I haven't arranged photography, but as soon as you approve this, we can move forward with—"

She's trying so hard, so determined to do this job well despite what's between us, and I love that about her.

Emotion surges in my pounding heart.

I try to stop it, but I can't—I'm falling in love with her.

21

QUINN

At the Bowery Mission on Friday, we make up a small group: me, Christian, and a single photographer. The photographer and I tuck ourselves into various corners of the kitchen and linger near the serving line for as long as it takes to get several photographs that will circulate online and in various press outlets.

I can't take my eyes off him.

He's so cocky, so self-assured, so self-centered. He uses women and then discards them seemingly by the week. He buys whatever he wants and never thinks twice about whether he deserves it. His money is all that matters to him.

At least, that's the image he projects most of the time. He lights up the room at the Purple Swan, charms his dates, tells dirty jokes—he's at the center of everything.

But at the Bowery, he's someone else.

The charm is still there, but it's warmer, softer, not so in-your-face. He speaks quietly to the people who move through the serving line, politely, in a welcoming tone. Everyone smiles at him as he dishes out portion after portion of steamed vegetables onto the waiting plates.

Even the way he moves is different, restrained somehow, as if he's fully aware of the power his body carries over people and is reining it in. He is graceful. Considerate. Humble.

He doesn't spare a look over at us, doesn't play up to the camera, not even once.

Christian is a natural.

The transformation is incredible to witness.

Even though he doesn't look at me, my eyes stay locked on him. I take the opportunity to study him without the laser focus of his eyes on mine—the cut of his jaw, the fullness of his lips, the sandy color of his hair.

He's mine.

No. He's not mine, and he may never be. A night of incredible sex does not a couple make, no matter how much I wish it was true when I lie in my bed without him by my side at night.

I watch him dishing up meals to people who need them, and something breaks open in my heart. It's a tiny shift, like a pebble falling down a mountain face, but for the first time since I found out about what Derek did, I glimpse a future where not every decision about men is a knee-jerk reaction based on his disgusting betrayal.

This is also the first time I've ever seen Christian's gentlemanly side. In front of my eyes, he is literally becoming a gentle man.

Not that I want a shy man. No. Not at all. The way we wrestle together in bed, the way he dominates me, it's something I've been craving for years without knowing it.

That's his real self, too.

I instinctively know it's true. In bed together on Tuesday, there was no need to posture. God knows I didn't. God knows I couldn't even stop myself from begging to be taken. That was raw. And the way he took me, again and again—that was absolutely him, down to the core.

Now I'm wondering which side of him—the party-obsessed playboy who views women as accessories or the quiet man in front of me—is the real Christian.

Maybe it's a pointless thing to think about. I'm not the same in every situation. He's not either. And when I think of his arrogance the day we first met—the way he practically commanded me to ride home with him—a shiver of pleasure runs down my spine. I can't get enough of him. I want *all* of him.

I nudge the photographer with my elbow. "Let's go."

"You don't want more shots?"

"Do you have three good ones?"

He glances at the screen on the back of his camera and gives me a confident nod.

"We're good. We'll meet him outside."

The photographer and I circle the block, and soon enough we're back outside the Mission with two reporters who are here to cover an announcement from Christian. I prepped him earlier this afternoon. I've engineered this entire event to look like it's rather spontaneous—you'd be surprised how little it matters if you call in the press—and like it comes straight from Christian's heart.

How he was acting inside, though...this cause is important to him.

There is more to Christian than meets the eye.

When I picture his face as he interacted with each person in the line, how he spoke to them as if they were of the same social class, acquaintances he was happy to see, the way his muscles worked and flexed as he served the food, my heart aches and warms at the same time.

Then it pounds.

It's way too early for this. I haven't even been able to completely disengage myself from that house in Colorado. I have the contractors texting me updates every day, and for one reason or another, things are being delayed.

I'd sell it for a loss if I had more savings, but I don't. Derek liked to travel, so we took the risk while we were still young and free.

Turns out that he was much freer than I was. What a dick.

I swallow the rage that's boiled up and shake my head to clear the negative thoughts. The point is, I can't be falling for Christian.

He comes out the entrance of the Bowery and I move toward him. A calm comes over me to see him.

It's absurd. It's true nonetheless.

"You were great in there," I say with a smile, my voice low.

Christian smiles back. "It was good."

"It was like you were a different person," I tease, as we walk toward the photographer, toward the reporters.

Something in Christian's face shifts abruptly. He's still smiling, but it doesn't look quite so real anymore. Am I imagining it, or is he shifting away from me?

What did I say?

I reach out for his arm, arrange my face as if I've remembered something important at the last moment. He turns toward me, his back to the press.

"Are you all right?" I keep my voice low.

"Yes," he says, his smile back. "I'm good."

"Did I say something wrong?" I can't let this thing between us affect my job, but if I don't fix whatever this is, I don't know how I can help him.

"Of course not," he says, but I don't believe him.

"I meant that it was amazing to watch you with those people. That's all I meant."

His face softens, relaxes, and my heart rate slows.

"I know that's what you meant," he says, softly, gently, and I know that if we weren't on the job, if there was no one around, he would lean down and kiss my cheek right now, cocky persona or not.

As he turns back toward the press, confusion zings through me. Is there something he's not telling me?

It doesn't matter. It can't destroy the way my heart sings when I look at him.

The emotion is deafening.

22

CHRISTIAN

My heart thunders in my chest as I turn away from Quinn and go to greet the press, and it continues to pound as I shake hands with the photographer and ask him about his gear. Then I chat with the reporters and mention casually that I'm making more time in my schedule to volunteer. I tell them that my mother did a lot of work while she was alive to try and lift people out of homelessness, and I want to honor her memory. At the last moment, I tack on that I'm making a rather large donation to the Bowery Mission.

The whole thing goes off without a hitch. A guy like me—like Christian Pierce—doesn't let one moment of awkwardness throw him off his game.

But something nags at me.

There's a pattern in myself that I don't like.

The things Quinn says are innocent. She doesn't know my secret. Intellectually, I know that, but every time she says something that brushes up against those boundaries, I react in a way that's impossible to hide.

Well, it's possible to hide it from other people, maybe. But I can't hide it from her.

How does she know how to read me so well?

We met each other last week, and already she can read me like we were born to be together. She even picks up on the subtle things that most of my other friends—even the closest ones—have never noticed, or if they did, they gave no indication of it.

My head is a mess.

I'm falling so hard for her and it's throwing me off-balance, out of control. I love it and hate it at the same time. I love that a woman has finally made me feel this way, but I hate that there's something inside me that will bring it all crashing to the ground.

It's time to get out of this.

It's a half-hearted thought. I'm barely *in* it yet.

I'm being torn in two, but I hide it while we walk to the Town Car.

Half of me wants to grab her right now and kiss her on the sidewalk, for all the world to see.

The other half of me wants to run in the opposite direction as fast and hard as I can and put Quinn Campbell far behind me.

She's a threat. There's no two ways about it. The way she reads me, the way she sees me, the way she is—it makes me want to be around her. Be with her. Be hers. Have her be mine.

And if *that* happens, I can't keep secrets from her.

Not the kind of secret that I've been keeping.

I can't.

Why not?

The little voice in my head wants to play devil's advocate again.

Why not? Why can't I have her, experience the greatest happiness I could ever experience in my life, and put the past behind me?

The answer comes immediately: because it will eat me alive.

I can't lie to her for the rest of my life. That kind of guilt would rot me from the inside out. And now, knowing what I know about Derek—knowing what I know about *Quinn* and the way she always demands honesty, even from herself—how could I do that to her?

We get into the Town Car, and as soon as I've closed the door behind me, Louis steers the car away from the curb.

"That was excellent," Quinn says lightly, looking down at her phone. "I'm not going to do a big push on this one because it will look too heavy-handed, but we'll get the photos circulating by tomorrow morning. You're bound to get a couple of low profile mentions, which is perfect for our purposes." She looks up at me and smiles. A little jolt of surprise runs through me. There's something in her eyes that wasn't there this morning. Part of it is confusion—after I got all fucking weird out there, she knows something's up but she doesn't know what—but part of it goes much deeper than that. She's practically glowing with it.

I want her to be close to me, even if it *is* a recipe for disaster.

"I'm looking forward to the next one," I tell her, both of us acting like it's important to maintain the facade in front of Louis.

For about twenty seconds.

That's as long as I last before I slide across the seat toward Quinn, wrap my arm around her, and pull her in for a hard, deep kiss.

"Wow," she says softly when I pull back to look into her eyes. "What did I do to deserve *that*?"

"Isn't it enough that I wanted it?"

"Wanted it?"

"Want you."

"I want you, too," she whispers in my ear.

"Come home with me."

"I can't."

I laugh out loud. That's Quinn Campbell—give her a direct order and she'll refuse.

Wait until I have her back in bed again.

"You *can*."

"I can't. I promised Carolyn I'd go for drinks with her as soon as this was over."

This is probably some kind of sign that I should take a

minute—a day, even—and get my mind right about this situation before I fuck up my entire life. "Okay."

Disappointment flickers across her eyes, but then she gives me a sultry smile. "Tomorrow, maybe?"

"We need to drop Quinn off at her place, Louis," I say. He gives me a jaunty salute in the rearview mirror and takes the next left.

~

Two hours later, I'm eating alone at the Purple Swan.

It's something I rarely allow myself to do. I'm already off-script for a Friday night. Instead of hosting a table full of loud assholes and gorgeous women in the main room, I'm seated in the smaller, more formal private dining room at a table for one.

All I can think about is Quinn.

All I can think about is how this ends.

All I can think about is how to get around having to end it, but there's no way to avoid it.

"Chris!" a voice booms behind me, and I turn to see my best friend in the city, Jax Hunter. He's been a busy guy lately now that he's married, and we haven't seen each other in a while. His wife, Cate, is on his arm. They're both beaming.

"Buddy!" I say, standing up and clapping him on the back. "How've you been? Where the hell are you these days?"

He and Cate share a conspiratorial look.

I don't get it at first, and then Jax gives Cate's still-flat belly a pointed look and raises his eyebrows at me.

"Are you kidding me?" I say with a big smile. Jax shakes his head. "Oh, my God—that's incredible news." I reach around Jax and give Cate a hug.

"What about you? You got that promotion, I see! Nice work."

"Oh, it was nothing," I joke. I'd love to sit down with Jax and tell him about Quinn, but he's already moving on.

"We'll see you around the club. Maybe not quite so often, though!" he tells me, and then I'm looking at their backs as they make their way to a round table next to the picture window at the back of the room.

My heart twists with jealousy.

Then at least one thing seems crystal clear: I could have what they have, and I could have it with Quinn.

I only need to figure out how.

23

QUINN

Christian is trying to make up his mind about something.

Maybe it's me.

After the Bowery appearance, Christian starts texting me—and not quick and dirty notes to plan our next rendezvous. In fact, he doesn't ask me to come to his apartment, not on Saturday, not even on Sunday.

At first, when the messages start coming in, I'm not sure what the hell is going on at all.

Tell me about you. How many siblings do you have?

None!

Only child?

Only child.

Must have been lonely.

When you're an only, your birthday budget is huge :)

You want a big birthday budget? ;)

I want a lot of things...I'm greedy.

The tone always turns flirty, with a strong undercurrent of desire, but he makes no indication that he wants me to come over. Sunday night goes by, and Monday, and Tuesday. Carolyn tells me he's at the Swan most nights, but she can't tell if he's taking a date with him or not. The woman I met that first time, Melody, is in some photos with him in the tabloids, but they're never touching—Christian walks ahead of her like he doesn't even see her.

Well, he's a grown man. He can do whatever he wants, as much as it stings.

Meanwhile, the messages keep coming.

Where are your parents from?

Michigan

Is that where you grew up?

Yeah, right in the middle.

What's it like there?

It's a few bigger cities surrounded by farmland. Everyone vacations up north

Should I go?

With me or alone?

Haha

It's not that he's disappeared. In fact, he does the opposite. He leans into my PR plan so aggressively that he even starts coming up with events to attend without me.

It makes me a little nervous that I don't have control over all of his appearances, but what can I do about it? Nothing. His free time belongs to him.

I wish more of it belonged to me. Then again...

I see him about every other day for our scheduled planning meetings. He sits across the desk from me, his eyes loitering over the curves of my body beneath the suit, the same smoldering half-smile on his face, but he doesn't lean over to whisper something filthy in my ear to make me wet right to the core. Then, on the way out, he'll catch me at the door, press me up against the wall, and kiss me like it's going to save him from drowning.

It's like we've gone back to the 1950s, but with cell phones. Suddenly, sex at his apartment is off the table completely—at least, he never mentions it. Suddenly, we're stealing kisses in the back of the Town Car, but when we reach our destination, he's distracted, disengaged.

I so badly want to ask him what's going on, but I can't. I can handle it if he's not into me anymore—if all of that was a fling, a fun distraction from real life—but I don't want to hear it. Not yet.

I decide to give myself until the house sells. When I'm finally free of it, I'll ask Christian what's going on.

If you could live anywhere in the world, where would you live?

Somewhere with great Wi-Fi

That's it?!?

That's my big requirement. I can do cities or small towns

The real question is...what are you going to do there?

There's a lot I'd like to do

I know

After the second media appearance, I'm jittery and distracted. I spent the entire time analyzing Christian's every glance at me. I get into the car and immediately his hands are on my face, pulling me toward him, devouring my mouth, savoring the flavor of our kiss.

It's so good, so *right*, that I don't think to call a halt to it and demand to know what the texting is about, demand to know why he hasn't taken me back to his place, demand to know where he stands on all of this. On us.

I don't understand this game we're playing.

Has he already moved on?

Was one time enough with me?

The doubt takes root and begins to flourish even as the messages keep coming, even while we have daylong conversations listing off the smallest details of our lives.

Though the contractors finish the repairs in the basement, it takes another week and a half to have it painted. There's a problem with the roof, and Sherrie thinks it's becoming a deal breaker for interested parties. If I could do some minor repairs in that area as well...

It frustrates me, but not as much as this bizarrely deep line of questioning from Christian. The fact that he wants to know so much about me is something I can't figure out. I like that he wants to know these things. I like that he sees me as a person and not a fuck toy. But why the sudden change in gears? Why via text?

After three weeks, my house hasn't sold, but I'm done.

I don't understand what he's doing, and when I've tried to guide the conversation there, he avoids it.

It's almost midnight on a Wednesday when I finally tell him that I can't do it anymore.

I send the text with shaking fingers and a pounding heart.

I want the heat between us.

I want the sex.

I want the domination.

I don't want endless text messages.

I can't keep having this conversation

Immediately, a bubble pops up on my screen. He's writing back.

My stomach turns over.

I can't either. Open the front door

I stand up from the couch, throwing the blanket that rested over my legs over the arm of the chair, and pad across the silent apartment to the front door. Carolyn went to bed early, exhausted from putting in too many hours today at her boutique. She needs to hire some more help, if you ask me. She can afford it. There's no reason to burn herself out.

I'm so tightly wound that my throat feels restricted.

I unlock the door and pull it open.

Christian stands in the hall, his hair damp from walking from his car to our building in the rain.

"Come in." I incline my head, ushering him into the entryway. Then I close and lock the door behind him. "Let's go to my room. Carolyn is sleeping."

He nods, and follows me through the apartment and down the hallway to my bedroom. I shut the door softly behind us, then round on him.

"What the hell?" I say, my voice sounding more tired than pissed off. "What happened? One day we're having sex that literally blows my mind, and the next you won't even talk about it?"

He takes a deep breath. "I had to figure some things out."

"Figure what out? What is it that we're even doing here?"

"I wanted to know more about you."

"And you couldn't take me on a date and ask me then?"

"Listen." He steps forward and takes my hand in his. "There's something I need to tell you."

The tension stretches thin between us and my stomach plummets into my shoes. What is he about to admit to me? That he's married? That he's found a girlfriend?

"I want to be with you."

I let out a laugh in spite of myself. "*What*?"

"I want to be with you, Quinn."

"I wanted to be with you for the past three weeks. What about then?" I'm half giddy, half hurt.

"I don't ever date women like you."

"I gather that."

"I never take women out on more than three dates."

I roll my eyes. "That's oddly specific. And bizarre."

"I know it is."

"So you didn't want to...waste the dates with me? That's why we've been sending messages by carrier pigeon?"

"That's what happened."

It hits me then: the look in his eyes, the way he's standing, shoulders curved toward me, the nervousness on his face. He's admitting to me the ridiculous reason why we haven't been spending every night together for the past three weeks.

He's *vulnerable.*

It sounds absurd, it sounds idiotic, but he's putting his real reputation as a confident playboy on the line to explain himself to me. My heart bursts.

He would never show this side of himself to someone he didn't trust.

I *knew* it. I *knew* it was more than sex.

Suddenly I'm grinning like an idiot, and all the weirdness of the past three weeks is forgiven.

"Are you done?" I say, unable to remove the smile from my face.

"Done with what?" he starts to smile, but doesn't seem to want to risk giving himself away unless I'm done being angry.

"Done with your stupid rules?"

"Yes," he nods, and I see it in his eyes—he's telling me the truth. He had to work things out. This was his way of giving us the chance to get to know each other, without the incredible distraction of wanting to fuck each other's brains out. I couldn't see it until right now.

"Thank God *that's* over," I cry, and then I'm clinging to him in his arms, our bodies pressed together, and his mouth is on mine, hot and needy and dominating, and everything is right with the world.

24

CHRISTIAN

She's forgiven me.

Thank God.

Something inside me breaks loose. It's freedom. It's seeing the light as you emerge from a dark room; it's like a ship gliding into its place at the dock, finally secure again after being tossed around on the ocean.

I couldn't bring her back to that place.

I couldn't do it.

As much as it terrifies me, the things she says, the memories she brushes up against when she speaks to me, I can't fake it like that. Not with her. Not any longer. That's off the table.

The more I learn about her, the more I see how strong she is. How fierce. How even in the face of uncertainty, she didn't lose her cool.

Not that I mind when she does, especially in bed.

I wish it hadn't taken so long for me to struggle with my choices.

After I saw Jax and Cate at the Swan, I knew that something had to change. I knew I was going to set aside my rules of engagement, set aside the fake penthouse, set aside all of it, and be with her.

She's probably right. I should have taken her on a date and asked her all the same questions, and I will. I absolutely will do that. But I had to pull back a little in order to come to terms with the magnitude of what's happening.

The magnitude of what I feel for her.

She's hot for me, ravenous for me, all over me. She claws at my clothes, tearing a couple of buttons loose in the process, and I can't wait another moment to see her body again. I pull her shirt roughly over her head and yank at the clasp of her bra, exposing her perfect breasts. She stifles a gasp with her hand when I lean down and take one of her nipples in my mouth, swirling my tongue around it, and then my hand is back on her neck, pulling her into me so I can taste her, show her that she's mine.

She's mine.

No matter what happens—no matter what kind of disaster this ends in—I'm not going to give up another second with her.

Still kissing her fiercely, I back her up and lift her onto the bed. She spreads herself wide for me and I can't help but grin for a moment before I start trailing wet kisses down over her breasts, down over her stomach, and then continue lower.

"Is this for me?" I say, putting a hand on either side of her hips.

Her eyes are black with desire, and I see something in them that I only see when we're together like this. When I drop my voice to use a certain tone with her. She's stripped down to another level, needing me, wanting me, wrestling with her own need to be in control.

"Yes," she whispers, and spreads her legs another inch apart, begging me without words to take her. To consume her. To claim her again and again.

It takes no words to give her what she wants.

I lean down and inhale her scent, then drag my tongue firmly over her soaking folds, lapping up the juices there.

She tastes amazing.

Quinn's body arches underneath me, her hips tilting up to press more of her against my face as I lick and suck and press my tongue into her wetness.

She presses her knuckles into her mouth to stifle her moans. It's difficult to remember, down here between her legs, that she has a roommate to be considerate of. Carolyn's been my friend for years, but right now I don't care if she hears us.

Quinn's desire rises to a fever pitch, her hips jerking as she comes into my mouth in another burst of sweetness.

Then I'm pulling her toward me, putting her on her feet, her legs still quivering, and I bend her over her bed, pressing her breasts into the soft covers.

"You're *mine*," I growl, and underneath my hands she moves, minuscule motion that signals to me that she agrees, she wants this, she loves this. Whatever way I choose to dominate her, she's prepared to take it.

I need to be in her.

Now.

I line myself up with her soaked slit and catch both of her wrists, pinning them at the small of her back. At the pressure of my hands on her wrists she lets out a deep moan, and in the sound is all her longing and need and a desperate request to fuck her, fuck her right now.

In one thrust, I'm buried deep in her wetness. There's not an ounce of resistance—she's so open for me that the only friction comes from the size of me pressing against her walls.

"*Yes*," she pants, the word a drawn-out hiss as I get into a rhythm, claiming her, for now, forever.

~

It's much later when the light of her phone screen wakes me up.

Quinn stands over near her vanity table, her hand cupped over the screen, squinting at it. I take a moment to look at her outline in the harsh white light emanating from the phone, at the tendrils of hair escaping from her bun, at the curve where her hip transitions into her waist.

Her shoulders slump and my heart twists to see it. Instantly I'm pushing the covers off, going to her side.

She leans into my touch, her head resting against my chest next to my tattoo.

"What's going on?" I ask her softly.

"My house in Colorado," she says, and then swallows hard. "It burned to the ground."

"Shit." Tears fill her eyes, but she's smiling now. "Quinn?"

"I'm free of it. I'm finally free of that place."

A smile spreads across my own face to see her relief. "Are you sure you're okay?"

"I'm great. I've never been better."

I lead her back to bed, pull her down into its softness with me, wrap her in my arms. She settles in, every muscle relaxing, safe and sound.

Several minutes later, as I'm starting to drift off, she says something I can't hear.

"What?" I whisper, not wanting to shatter the peace of the moment.

"I love you."

My heart nearly flies out of my chest. It's never felt more right to hear those words. We'll talk about all of this, figure out our next steps, decide for ourselves if it's too early, but for right now...

I smooth my hand over her hair and squeeze her one more time. "I love you, too, Quinn."

25

QUINN

My heart hasn't felt this light and free in months, maybe years. Now that there's nothing holding me back in Colorado, it's like a massive weight has been lifted.

The house is a total loss, and so Thursday is eaten up with strategic planning for Christian's next wave of public appearances and phone call after phone call from my insurance company. It seems like they're calling every hour on the hour to confirm various details with me—how much furniture was left in the house, the accuracy of my home inventory list, how much I have left to pay on the mortgage.

"Ms. Campbell?"

I answer the phone for the twentieth time. It's never joyful to deal with an insurance company, but I'm over the moon—and not because of the house.

"Yes?"

"This is Michael Deacon, calling from Mountainside."

"Hi, Michael."

"I wanted to call and give you an update on your claim."

"It's—" Wait. He hasn't asked me for another list, another confirmation. "Really?"

"Yes. Could you confirm some identifying details for me for security purposes?"

"Of course." I rattle off my mother's maiden name, my birthdate, and my social security number for hopefully the last time today.

"Thank you, Ms. Campbell. I'm calling to inform you that the preliminary decision on your claim is that the mortgage company will be reimbursed according to..."

I'm so swept away by what happened last night, and so worn down by the constant phone calls, that Michael's voice becomes a blur. I snap back into awareness as he says:

"...of course, this is pending a final walkthrough of the site by one of our inspectors. Someone has already been out to visit the property today, but you should see resolution in the next thirty to sixty days."

Perfect. All of this means they'll be sending paperwork, and then I can read the fine print on my own time, when my head isn't swimming with love and lust.

"Thanks for the update, Michael. Is there anything else you need from me?"

"Nope. Thanks for choosing Mountainside for your home insurance needs."

"No problem. Goodbye."

I hang up the call and slide my phone back into my purse, and then I lean back against my seat, relief flooding my body.

From what I understand, most of the payout will go to my mortgage holder, with a small amount left over for me. I wouldn't care if I got nothing—the sweet unburdening I feel from not having to deal with this house and all its attendant problems anymore is nearly overwhelming. I can always wait to sell the property. Or have Sherrie list it for such an absurdly cheap price that developers won't be able to resist. They never stay away forever, even after a wildfire.

But the thing that has my heart singing, bursting, soaring is Christian's words last night.

My own declaration to him slipped out unbidden as I was on the edge of sleep and basking in the unbelievable comfort of being held in his arms, under a cascade of relief from hearing the news about my house. At first, when he whispered, "what?" I thought I might be dreaming, and Dream Quinn had no reservations about telling a man she's only known for a month or so that she loved him.

When the words were out of my mouth a second time, less garbled and sleepy, something in me froze. It was *real.*

I felt him take a deep, quick breath. I didn't open my eyes.

Then he ran a hand over my hair and said, so softly, "I love you, too, Quinn."

Heat screams across my cheeks whenever I think about it.

There's nothing holding me back in Colorado. Everything is beginning here in New York City.

It's enough to make any girl giddy, but I resolve to play it cool. It was late at night, when we said those things to each other, and nearly asleep. People *say* things late at night. You can't always hold them to it the next morning.

A smile plays across my face. Those words had the ring of truth, though. So even if we don't speak them again for a while, I know they're waiting in the wings.

I'm sure they are.

I leave the office that night still floating on cloud nine and spend the ride home texting Christian flirty messages. He's at some kind of event with his father on behalf of Pierce Industries, and I have plans with Carolyn.

She's waiting when I get back to the apartment.

"Hey!" she says from the kitchen. Something smells wonderful.

"Hey! Are you cooking?"

"Baking," she answers, laughing. "Your house burning down calls for cake."

"You can't go wrong with cake," I say, and go to open a bottle of wine.

Over takeout and chocolate cake, Carolyn considers me. "You're in an awfully good mood for someone whose house was destroyed. Weren't you trying to sell it?"

I groan a little. "It was an unbelievable pain in the ass, Care.

It would have been nice to have the money, but not thinking about it...it's priceless."

"Is that *all* that's going on with you? You're practically glowing."

It's hard to get anything past Carolyn.

"Christian and I...might be taking things to the next level."

"*Might* be?" she says, her voice rising in pitch.

I can't help but laugh. I love that about her. "Things got a little weird for a couple of weeks, but he came over last night..."

"Wait. Christian was *here*, and neither of you told me?"

"It was late."

Understanding dawns in her eyes. "You little minx."

My abs are sore from laughing, but the words out of Carolyn's mouth send me into another fit of giggles. "Yeah... what do you want from me?" I take a sip of wine and smile at her. "I think we're going to *date*."

Concern crosses her face. "What about your job?"

"It's going to stay a secret."

"That won't be easy. Christian's pretty high-profile."

"It doesn't have to be secret *forever*."

"If you're okay with it..." She brightens up. "You're not afraid to get fired?"

"Oh, I'm *totally* afraid to get fired." My mood turns serious. "But Car—I can't let this go. I know he's a womanizer and a playboy, but there's something...there's something else there. I can't give up the chance to find out what it is, where it may lead. You know?"

"I know," my roommate says, her eyes sparkling. "I've never heard of him going to a woman's place before," she comments, a note of wonder in her voice. "You could be *the one*."

26

CHRISTIAN

I feel so good as I'm tiptoeing out of Carolyn's apartment in the early hours of Thursday morning that I almost forget that this thing with Quinn—this mind-blowing, heart-stopping thing with Quinn—is bound to crash and burn. We're speeding toward the inevitable fallout the moment I tell her the truth about what happened that fateful night.

I walk a block and a half before Louis pulls up to the curb. I didn't give him much warning, but the guy's a professional. He doesn't so much as rub—or roll—his eyes.

I collapse into the back seat and let everything wash over me.

It felt so perfect to lie there with Quinn resting gently against my chest, my arms wrapped around her lithe body. In that moment, there was nothing standing between us. She was mine to protect, although I'm learning every day that she doesn't need protection. I've never met a woman who can bounce back like she can.

And she was willing to jump in with both feet, despite the way things have been going the past couple of weeks.

The truth is that I needed time to make the shift.

Nobody's going to think anything of it.

I've taken a few weeks off from my nightly trips to the Swan, only going there once or twice every week, and never with a date. At least, not one that I take home at the end of the night. Sooner or later someone's going to ask what happened to the Christian Pierce who gleefully adds notches to his belt without a second thought. I've long since lost count of the women who have sat by my side at the Swan for three dates and then never seen there again.

At least this way, it won't be a sudden shock. At least this way, when word gets out that I'm seeing someone—and it will get out—they'll look back and see that I wasn't quite so active at the Club, and they'll chalk it up to a new obsession, maybe even real love.

Real love.

That's what I confessed to Quinn last night, consequences be damned, and now, as Louis steers the car through the predawn gray of the morning, I don't regret a word of it. Instead, my heart pounds with a kind of electric thrill. It's the kind you only feel when you stumble upon something so true, so deep, that to lie about it would be unthinkable.

I rub at my forehead.

Here I am, back at the thorn in my side. The one thing that's going to bring us crashing back to earth.

Don't tell her.

It's the obvious solution, right? I could keep my secret buried deep inside, like I have for the past decade. I could let it fade away into memory, take it to the grave with me, like I was planning to do before Quinn came along and changed everything.

Louis hits the gas and I flash back to that party.

I was drunk, but not that drunk—and not high, like my brother. Cheap beer, a shot or two—I paced myself, like I always did. I was always the responsible one. Always the one who held back a little, just in case.

The music was loud, but not so loud that it would draw any attention. Not that the police ever stopped by this building anyway. Too many wealthy apartment owners stacked one on top of the other, all the way up to the penthouse—it was always a waste of time to investigate, a waste of time to prosecute.

I don't know how late it was by the time everyone filtered out, stumbling off in high heels and short skirts. My brother had invited the best of the best from our class, children of investment bankers and owners of corporations rivaling Pierce Industries. Some of them were far more adventurous than I ever was, going to underground parties that routinely got busted by the cops. It didn't matter. Money could buy you out of anything.

That's what I thought until the silence in the apartment set in.

Where was my brother?

Where had he gone?

My mind in a haze from the alcohol, I tried to remember if

he had been with a girl that evening. He'd been talking to several, his arm around one girl's shoulders, whispering in her ears, that signature grin on his face—but had he taken her into one of the bedrooms? The last thing I wanted was to walk in on him while they were in the middle of the act.

At first I tried to dismiss the heavy silence as nothing, but it pounded at my ears until I forced myself up from the sofa and went to find him, straining to hear anything that might clue me in to his whereabouts.

The first bedroom was empty.

The second bedroom was playing host to a couple sprawled out on the bed, passed out, but neither person was my brother.

Dread settled into the pit of my stomach as I made the long walk to the master bedroom at the end of the hall.

My first thought when I pushed the door open was that the room was empty. It was that quiet.

I stepped inside, heart hammering against my rib cage, and glanced around. The lamp atop the dresser was on, and the comforter on the bed was rumpled.

Nobody there.

I crossed to turn off the lamp, and with my hand on the switch, started to turn back toward the door.

That's when I saw his hand, limp and white on the carpet. It was all I could see of him until I stepped around to the other side of the bed, where his body was crumpled against the box spring...

"Mr. Pierce?"

"Yes?" Louis must have said my name more than once.

"We're here."

"Thanks."

I slide out of the car and shake it off, force away the cold, sick feeling that I get when that memory overtakes me. Immediately, Quinn's face swims up before my eyes, and a burst of warmth and love fills my chest.

I'm going to start by showing her the way I *live*, not that stripped-down apartment I use for hookups.

She's so much more than that to me now.

I'm going to do this even though the thought sends a wave of cold fear through my body.

I'm deep into making plans by the time I walk through the door of my building.

I'm going to start with my place in the Hamptons.

This is where our love story begins.

27

QUINN

Friday is another dry spell I don't have a single meeting with Christian scheduled.

On the one hand, it makes it easier to build out my plans for him since he's not here to distract me with those eyes and that body.

On the other hand, even though he's not here in person, all I can think of are his eyes—the way the black of his pupil is ringed by a lightning strike of blue so light that it's almost pure white. It reminds me of the way the ocean waves exploded outward from the shore in various shades of blue, ringing around a tropical island I once visited with my parents when I was a teenager. Christian's eyes are a different color of blue, changing from moment to moment, depending on the light, his mood...

Now that I'm intimately acquainted with his body, that's hard to forget, too. I'm as professional as they come, but when he's sitting across from me, his ripped abs hidden by a crisp white shirt and topped by a slim-cut jacket that does nothing but emphasize the hard line of his waist...

I shake my head and loosen my grip on the computer mouse. It's one thing to catch yourself rubbing your thighs against one another underneath your desk at work. It's another to completely abandon your job to go masturbate in the bathroom.

My heart thunders in my chest. It's so dangerous to be with Christian. I could lose my job if anyone were to find out. I *don't* want to get fired from HRM. Not now that I have no safety net back in Colorado, and not when I'm finally making big strides in my career. A ruined reputation is no joke.

But how can I stay away from him?

I bite my lip as I maneuver some of the events around on his calendar.

The answer is that I can't.

I can't.

I don't want to.

And I won't.

We'll proceed cautiously, and not because of my job. It seems like a long time ago now, but it hasn't been long since I had my heart shattered and then stomped on and spat on by that bastard Derek. Christian might have a tenderhearted side, but there's no guarantee he's good right to the core.

My body heats up at the thought of him. I'm trying to be rational, but what I'm feeling isn't a rational emotion. I know we're right together—at least right now.

Day by day, Quinn. Day by day.

It's after 5:00, and I'm making the last few changes to next week's schedule when my phone vibrates in my purse.

When I pick it up, the sight of Christian's name sends my heart rate skyrocketing.

Head over heels, for sure.

Run away with me.

Right now???

I want to show you the real me.

Haven't I met you before??

I'm waiting outside in the car. You're not working late on a Friday

Is that a question? :)

It's an order ;)

A shiver runs down my spine. He might be joking, but imagining the kind of orders a man like Christian could give turns me *on*. Even if I'm the kind of woman who's not the sweet, submissive type. Sex is like a battle between us, and that's how I like it.

I'll get my things together...

Don't linger, my love

I stop dead at the words on the screen, my breath hitching in my throat. It's not quite an *I love you*, but it's close.

I leave the office at a measured pace, because it's not very seemly for a senior reputation manager to sprint out of the room, fling herself into a waiting Town Car, all while tearing off her clothes in the process, which is exactly what I'd like to do right now.

I stand calmly in the elevator as it whisks me down to the lobby, and I even take the time to tuck my access badge into my purse and put on my sunglasses before exiting the building.

The Town Car is parked right in front of the HRM headquarters. Louis stands outside the back door, waiting to open it for me. After a quick glance to the left and right to make sure no one is watching, I'm striding across the hot pavement. With a nod to Louis, I slip into the cool, leather-filled interior of the Town Car.

Christian's hands are on me in an instant, and he only takes them off to punch a button on the side of the car.

"What—" I start to say, and then his mouth is on mine, and I'm lost in his kiss, drowning in desire as a partition goes up between us and Louis. It's the first time Christian has ever used it.

We're pulling away from the curb before he breaks the kiss and smiles broadly at me, his eyes sparkling in the afternoon sun.

"Wow," I say breathlessly.

"Run away with me." He repeats the words from the text message as if I hadn't already agreed to come.

"I am—aren't I?"

"I can still drop you off at home."

"Don't do that. Wait—where are we going? Shouldn't I get clothes?"

"You don't need clothes." He gives me a wicked look.

I want to bite at his lip, kiss him harder, and so I do. When we come up for air, I continue the conversation. "I'll need clothes at some point."

"What I *meant* was," he replies, his voice smooth and sexy and confident, "I have clothes for you where we're going."

I look toward the ceiling of the Town Car and shake my head a little in bewilderment. "You're such a...such a..."

"Billionaire?" His half-smile lights me up from head to toe.

"What if I want my own clothes?"

He leans over to whisper in my ear, despite the partition. "You won't be thinking about clothes for long once we're there."

I suck in a deep breath, shudders of pleasure running rampant through my body. "Where's there?"

"Do you want me to ruin the surprise?"

"What I *meant* was, how long is the ride?"

"Two hours."

"How soundproof is that partition?"

He answers me with his tongue.

28

CHRISTIAN

I spread Quinn out on the backseat, hiking her skirt right up around her waist and pulling her panties down to her knees, and delve into the hot slit between her legs, licking and lapping and tasting until I've worked her into a frenzy.

I would bet that under normal circumstances Quinn would be a stickler for wearing seat belts, but five minutes under the attentions of my tongue and her eyes are closed and her hands clench involuntarily, moving in rhythm with the pulsing motions of her pussy. I feel the movements under my tongue and my cock, already hard from watching her hips sway as she walked across the sidewalk toward the car, strains against my pants, pulsing impatiently.

We're still crawling along in Friday rush-hour traffic, creeping slowly through Manhattan, when I wipe my mouth with my sleeve and pull her to a sitting position, pressing her back up against my side. I hold her there, tightly, with one arm while my other hand explores her breasts, diving inside her shirt to tweak her nipples as she writhes against me.

"What are you *doing* to me?" she gasps, trying to turn to face me. I only press her harder against me.

"Driving you crazy," I murmur into her ear, and then I slide my hand down between her legs.

She's soaking wet, her folds soft and perfect, and in three strokes I have her going again. It's as if the shuddering orgasms she had while I devoured her never happened, or as if they happened but only made her need *more.*

I circle her clit with my fingertips, softly at first, then harder, increasing the speed until she's right on the brink, and then I pull my hand away. She inhales sharply and I clap my hand over her mouth in time to catch her scream of frustration and lust in my palm. Quinn pants against my skin as I dip my fingers into her folds again, thrusting two into her opening and drawing them in and out. She spreads her legs as wide as she can, given the constraints of her panties, and I seize the moment.

Reaching down, I shove her panties toward her shins, and she wriggles her legs so that they slide off, ditching her heels in the process. Then, with one motion, I lift her, turn her, so that she's straddling me.

She kisses me with such heat that it's a genuine surprise the car doesn't burst into flames. I *love* this—the way she uses her entire body to pin me back against the seat, the way she presses her weight against me, driving her hips into my pelvis.

Quinn pulls back, then leans in again to catch my earlobe

between her teeth. I can't stop the groan that escapes my mouth. How does she know to do that? It doesn't matter. I want her to keep going, and then I want to fuck her until...

Dragging her mouth down my jawline, she leaves a hot, wet trail down the side of my neck, then shifts her weight backward as she reaches for my belt. Her face is focused, eyes heavy and glittering with lust, pupils dilated, and she dispatches the belt with the same dogged efficiency that she uses in the office. My zipper is next, and then I lift my hips toward her so she can tug my pants down around my thighs.

I catch her hands in midair as she reaches for me, and with my fingers curled around each of her wrists, I spread her arms wide, leaning in.

She's wearing a pale pink button-down top with her now-rumpled pencil skirt, and I take the topmost button between my teeth and give it a sharp jerk. She cries out a little when it pops off. I'm not going to apologize for destroying one top in the name of pleasure. Two buttons, three, and her lacy bra is exposed, her breath causing her breasts to rise into my face, the smooth skin against my close-shaven jawline.

Quinn looks straight into my eyes, and her mouth curves into a smile so carnal-laced that my cock starts throbbing again. Then she jerks both of her wrists, freeing them from my hands. Not another second passes before her mouth is on mine and she's lined up her pussy over my cock and fuck, *fuck*, thrust herself downward, taking all of me inside her hot channel in one swift movement.

She fucks me furiously, relentlessly, a delicate sheen of sweat rising at her hairline as she works herself up and down over me, taking me in so deeply I bottom out, making contact with her ridged barrier over and over.

It's like she can't stop herself, and in thirty seconds I'm nearing the edge. She digs her fingers into my shoulders and slams into me, slams, *slams*, harder, *harder*, her pussy clenching around me in rhythmic spasms. She kisses me when she comes, lips parted, moaning into my mouth, and I swallow her pleasure, letting it push me right up to the edge, so close to it that I can't stop myself...

At the very last possible moment Quinn thrusts herself off of me and backward and sinks down to her knees on the floor of the Town Car, taking me into her mouth, sucking in as I explode, my hips jerking back and forth. She takes it all.

When I'm finished, she looks up at me, her expression satisfied, and wipes the back of her hand across her mouth. Then she clambers back onto the seat next to me and tucks her legs under her. I gather her under my arm, and she rests her head against my heaving chest.

"Fuck," she whispers softly, and I have no words to respond, my mind has been so thoroughly blown by my girlfriend.

My girlfriend.

That's what she is now, even though we haven't said it out loud.

I take a deep breath and kiss her temple.

As soon as we get to my place in the Hamptons—and as soon as I can catch my breath—it's time to start letting her in.

29

QUINN

Once we've both recovered from our backseat escapade—I pull an emergency tank top out of my purse, then insist on some belated seatbelt safety—Christian starts telling me about where he's taking me.

"In case you haven't guessed, we're going to the Hamptons."

"The Hamptons," I repeat, tasting the richness of the word in my mouth.

Christian leans forward and opens a compartment tucked under the front seat to reveal a cooler full of ice. Nestled in the center is a bottle of champagne. From somewhere else he produces a corkscrew and opens the bottle. Two champagne glasses emerge from a second compartment located under the passenger seat. While he pours out the liquid bubbly, his hand not wavering at all despite the movement of the car, he continues.

"My father originally bought the cottage as a family vacation home, and growing up we spent the summers there. Some weekends in the fall, too. My mother—" He swallows thickly and keeps his gaze focused on the champagne glasses as he passes one over to me. "My mother loved it there. After they divorced, he wanted to sell it, but I convinced him to hold on to the property. I bought it from him when I got full access to my trust fund. That was the best thing about turning twenty-five."

"The best thing? Not the incredible party I'm sure you had?"

He flicks his eyes over to me, a little smile playing on his lips. "When I turned twenty-five, I had the same party I always have. Dinner at the Swan. Drinks. Dancing. Women."

Something in his tone tells me it's not the party he wanted. I don't quite understand it, because the last time I saw Christian at the Swan, he was in his element.

"Where did you want to be instead?"

He lets out a breath that's not quite a sigh. "Elsewhere."

"Tell me." I take a sip of the champagne, its bubbly sweetness sparkling on my tongue. "Where?"

Christian sips at his own champagne, then turns to look at me, his chin lifted. "That was a tough birthday."

My cheeks flame red as I remember—Christian's brother. How the fuck could I have forgotten that little detail? "Oh, my God," I say, slapping a hand to my forehead. "I'm so sorry. I can't believe I—"

"It's all right," Christian says quickly, but I see a flash of something I can't identify in his eyes. It doesn't look like grief. That's all I know, and then it's gone. "I always held the party at the Swan because..." His mouth works. When he speaks again, something is different about his voice. "My brother was always the quiet one, but I think he liked the parties we would throw together." A pinprick of icy unease forms on the back of my neck. Why? Something rings false.

Then again, what the hell do I know? The entire point of this vacation, if Christian's text is to be believed, is to give me a chance to see the reality of his life. It makes perfect sense, after all—the Swan isn't exactly the kind of place to get to know someone's deep secrets, and there's not much more to my life than Carolyn's apartment at the moment.

I dismiss the feeling. Christian clears his throat. The silence has gone on for too long.

I give him a comforting smile and reach across to take his hand in mine. "No need to talk about that if you don't want to."

"I do want to." Suddenly his face is open, his eyes almost pleading, and yet his tone is forceful. He's not the kind of guy to cede control of a situation. "I want you to know everything there is to know about me."

"I want that, too," I say carefully. The conversation has taken an intense turn, and Christian's eyes, crystal blue in the filtered light coming through the Town Car's windows, bore into mine.

"I mean it."

"I know."

There's a strange energy crackling between us, and it makes me both intrigued and slightly uncomfortable at the same time. I've never seen this side of him.

Then the moment fades, and Christian shakes his head, a little, sexy half-smile on his face.

"I don't mean to freak you out," he says finally, and I let out a little laugh of relief.

"Jesus Christ, I hope not," I say, and then it's his turn to laugh. It's a good thing we're going to spend the weekend getting comfortable before we dive into anything serious.

It's already serious, says the voice in the back of my mind. I can't argue.

"What about you?"

"What about me?" I say, giving him a coy smile.

"Any special places you want to tell me about?"

"Not a cottage in the Hamptons, that's for sure."

He laughs, not unkindly. "Where did you vacation?"

"Anywhere," I say. "Everywhere. My parents were camper people."

"Camper people?" Christian looks mildly confused.

"They liked to haul a pop-up camper behind their car. That's where we'd stay when we went on vacation."

"Oh," says Christian thoughtfully. "I don't think I'm the camper type."

"No?"

"That doesn't seem like it would be...sturdy."

"They're plenty sturdy."

"Not for the kinds of things I'd like to do to you on vacation."

I suck in my breath, heat rising again between my legs, and then I bite down on my bottom lip. "Not fair."

"It's the truth."

In front of us, the partition lowers. Without taking his eyes off the road, Louis calls back to Christian. "We're here, Mr. Pierce. Should I drop you off in front?"

"Great."

I look out the window. The winding drive we're on is large enough, and long enough, to be an actual road, which is what I assumed we were traveling on until this moment. Then Louis pulls the car around a circular drive in front of an honest-to-God mansion.

My mouth drops open. I should have expected this, but I was so caught up in our...*activities*...and then our conversation that I didn't bother to ask how big this place was. I look back at Christian, who is smiling, his eyes shining with pride and anticipation.

"The cottage," he says.

Sure, I think, too excited to admit out loud. *This is a cottage, and I'm a princess!*

30

CHRISTIAN

Quinn steps inside the front entry to the cottage—she's right, the name is possibly the biggest understatement in history—like she's entering a castle, or a cathedral. The brickwork and the soaring windows contribute to the effect, and so does the fact that the staff has lined up in the foyer to greet us.

It's not a large staff, but Quinn's eyes widen nonetheless.

"This is Robert, the chef," I say, introducing her to the stocky man who is dark and handsome, although not very tall. He shakes Quinn's hand with a mischievous twinkle in his eye. "Rosemary, the housekeeper." Rosemary steps forward, her grandmotherly vibe putting Quinn at ease. "We also have a gardener who's here three days a week, and of course you know Louis." At that moment, Louis appears from a side entrance carrying two suitcases, then disappears up the grand staircase with a nod.

"Rosemary, Robert, this is Quinn."

"I'm so—I'm so pleased to meet you," Quinn says, blushing

a little. She must feel out of her element, to let a little thing like meeting my staff throw her off. This is nothing—*nothing*—like the apartment I took her to. That might as well be a hotel for all the personality it has.

"Lovely to meet you, as well," Rosemary replies in return, beaming at Quinn. "She's lovely, Mr. Pierce."

"Thank you, Rosemary," I say, and then, with a nod, I let them go back to their business.

Robert lingers for one more moment. "I have a late dinner prepared for the both of you, Mr. Pierce. Would you like Rosemary to bring it up to your suite in about an hour?"

"Wonderful."

"Excellent," Robert says, then turns on his heel and hurries back in the general direction of the kitchen.

Alone at last, I turn to Quinn, who's still gazing around her like she's in a foreign country. "Would you like a tour?"

"*Yes*," she says with a definitive nod. "I have got to see this place. This is incredible."

I show her the formal dining room, which has a table large enough to seat twenty-four people, the downstairs library, and the formal living room. We peek into the kitchen, where Robert is busy putting the finishing touches on our meal, and Quinn glances across at me. "Those are some seriously fancy appliances."

I shrug. "My father had them installed before he and my mother got divorced. She liked to moonlight as a baker when she wasn't attending charity events and fighting with him about how much he liked to party with his friends."

"Is that where you get it from?"

She's teasing, but something twists in my chest.

Because the truth is....*the truth is*...

I pull myself back from the brink. No. Now is not the moment to try and bring that up. The weekend is beginning. Our relationship is beginning. It's going to be crucial not to be too hasty.

"Come on," I say, tilting my head back toward the main part of the house. "There's a lot more to see."

Upstairs, I lead her down the hallway to the master suite—another understatement. There are eleven guest rooms, but the master suite—the rooms I occupy whenever I'm here—includes a massive bedroom, two walk-in closets, a den, and a small study.

"Holy shit," Quinn says, her voice almost a whisper, as I push the door and it swings open noiselessly on its hinges.

Unlike my apartment, this room is full of personal things.

"So, this is my room."

"Your *room*."

"My rooms."

Family photos appear on almost every shelf, and the decorator I hired incorporated lot of smaller touches—my college degree, framed, hangs between two bookshelves, the armchair sitting underneath it practically begs you to put your feet up. My books occupy most of the other shelf space.

Something in Quinn's face shifts as she sees it all, and like a moth drawn to a light, she moves away from me and toward all the things out in front of her in plain sight.

Right away Quinn notices a shelf filled with leather-bound journals at waist level behind the armchair. “Christian,” she says, with a note of wonder in her voice. “Do you keep a *diary*?”

“I kept *journals*,” I say, grinning at her, but then the words stick in my throat. What the hell should I say now that won’t give me away? My heart skips, wrenches. Why is it like this? Why is it that one moment I’m fine, enjoying her company, letting this unfold how it’s going to unfold, and then the next minute I’m seized by such a frigid dread that it almost takes my breath away?

You want this.

The thought floats up into my mind. It’s true. I want her. I want all of her. Now, tomorrow, forever.

Carefully.

Carefully.

She doesn’t notice when the smile falls away from my face. She’s too busy looking at the first editions of the classics on the rest of the shelves.

“Damn,” she says quietly.

“There’s more in the den, if you’re interested.”

She turns back to me, and flicks the tip of her tongue out to lick her lips. “You know,” she says, “I seem to remember Robert saying Rosemary would be up in an hour. How long do we have left?”

I glance down at my watch. “Fifteen minutes.”

Quinn’s hands are already working at the straps of her tank top, pulling it over her head. She is insatiable.

The bedroom is down a narrow hallway, tucked away in the back of the suite. In two steps I’m next to her, my arm around her waist, and as she’s unhooking the clasp of her bra and tugging it off, I’m leading Quinn to my massive bed.

When she sees the king-size masterpiece, impeccably made up, she gives a little sigh of pleasure. “It’s impressive,” she comments, then turns and starts to unbutton my shirt. “But not as impressive as you.”

31

QUINN

What happens on Christian's bed can't be described as making love. It's a quick and dirty fuck, with me on top, but we have a lot more room than we did in the Town Car.

When we've finished, I sprawl out on the bed and wait for my heart rate to quiet down and my breathing to slow.

"That...was incredible."

"It's always incredible with you."

I roll over and kiss his cheek. "You're too sweet."

"I was thinking about something in the car."

"What?"

He turns on his side to look into my eyes, and I mirror him. In this moment, at least, I don't see a flicker of doubt.

"We need to come up with a title for what we are."

My heart skips a beat, then it speeds up. Are we going to talk about this *now*?

"Like, Lord and Lady Pierce?" I say, letting out a nervous laugh. I didn't know how badly I wanted Christian to bring this up until he did, and now that he has, I'm for some reason afraid that the moment will slip away.

He grins at me. "If you want. But my thoughts were more along the lines of...introducing you as my girlfriend."

I can't wipe the smile off my face. "I do," I joke, echoing hypothetical wedding vows. I'm only half kidding, but I'll never admit it.

Christian bursts out laughing, the sound deep and musical. "I remember what we said the other night. It's still true for me. Is it true for you?"

"Yes," I say, my expression turning serious. "It doesn't make sense, but it's still true." Truth or not, I can't bring myself to say the words again. I'm too consumed by the jitters. The tattoo on his bare chest catches my eye, and I spend a few seconds tracings its curves and lines with my gaze. It's an intricate coat of arms, the thick lines dark on his skin, and the design is divided into different sections, each with an image inside. Something pricks at the back of my mind. Something is off about it, but I can't put my finger on what it is.

"We can't be public, though. My job—"

"I know. We'll work it out."

"Good." I let out a breath. I'm still not willing to give up my job over this. Maybe if we were *married*...nah, I'd still want to work. I'm not the stay-at-home type.

"You don't think it makes sense?"

"No," I say, rolling over onto my back. Christian slides across the bed, and then traces a finger over my jawline. "We just met, and I'm barely out of my last long-term relationship, and you're a playboy who—"

"Prove it."

"Oh, stop. You're at the Swan almost every night with a different woman!"

"I haven't been."

"Since when?"

"Since you."

His deep blue eyes are locked on mine. Maybe it doesn't matter that all this happened fast. Being together is the most important thing. I'm complete. Perfect.

Except…

I glance around Christian's bedroom, at the expensive, heavy furnishings, spotless and neatly arranged. Then I look back into his eyes. "I'm not like you, though."

A muscle twitches in his cheek, and again there's that strange energy, that sensation that tells me I might have hit a nerve. I don't see how I could…

"How so?" His question comes a bit too late.

"I'm not rich!" I push myself up to sitting against the pillows piled against the headboard. "I'm pretty sure this cottage is actually a castle." I give the word "cottage" air quotes, and Christian's face is instantly relaxed again.

"That doesn't matter to me."

"What does matter to you?"

He presses his lips together thoughtfully. "There's something about you that I can't ignore. When you're in the room, my attention is drawn to you. You're so...you're so confident, so sure of yourself, so hot..." Christian plants several kisses down the side of my neck, then pulls back. "I can trust you."

"I'm pretty sure I can trust you, too."

His reaction is instant, and it's only a flash, but I see it—fear. It's not something that often appears on Christian's face.

"What was that?"

"What?" he says, his half-smile already back in place.

"You looked..." I don't want to embarrass him. I don't want to be the kind of woman who comes on a romantic getaway with a man and then hounds him for every single questionable expression that crosses his face. "You looked a little freaked out for a second." I try to lighten the moment. "Maybe I'm seeing things. That kind of vigorous sex we had can play tricks on your mind."

"I'm not afraid," he says, his voice even and calm. "I'm—I want you to be sure you can trust me." He raises his hands, indicating the room. "That's why we're here. I want you to see how I live."

"Are you telling me you don't always live in your apartment?"

"I almost never live there."

I shoot him a look. That apartment was pretty nice.

"That's...more of a crash pad. I spend most of my nights at my penthouse in Midtown."

Understanding dawns slowly in my mind. "Wait. You have a separate apartment to bring women to?"

He doesn't hesitate. "Yes."

I consider Christian's face carefully. He doesn't look ashamed to tell me this, and he shouldn't be. He's rich enough to have several places to stay. The crucial element here is that he's being honest with me about it.

My heart warms, glows. He's telling me everything, even the things that come off as a little bit unsavory.

This is the real deal.

"Well...as long as you can afford the rent."

We both laugh at that one, and then he puts a hand to the side of my face. "You should know that I haven't brought anyone there since we met."

I put my hand to the side of his face. "You should know that was a smart choice, Christian Pierce."

"Once you've met the right woman, everyone else pales in comparison."

"Damn right." I lean in and kiss him, softly, my tongue playing over his lips, then slipping into his mouth. "Any other secret apartments you want me to know about?"

"I own several other properties around the city. I'll take you to all of them if you'd like."

"But they don't mean much to you."

"No. They're much like the apartment we were in together." He grins wickedly. "The real action happens in my penthouse."

"When will you take me there?"

"Whenever you want."

"Okay," I joke, swinging my legs over the side of the bed. "Let's go."

Christian wraps an arm around my waist, pulling me back down to the comforter. "With dinner on its way up? Not a chance."

Then his mouth is on mine, and I've forgotten all about being funny.

32

CHRISTIAN

For the next two days, I show Quinn firsthand what life is like at the Pierce Cottage in the Hamptons.

I start with the wardrobe I've had selected for her. Rosemary has arranged it in the closet of the guest suite right next to my room. Not that she'll be sleeping anywhere but right by my side. This way, she'll have a private place to dress and shower in the morning—if she wants it. Quinn spends a full fifteen minutes in the walk-in closet filled with clothes in her size, something for every occasion, from yoga pants to evening dresses. It doesn't matter that we're only staying for a couple of days. We can do anything we want while we're here.

"You almost got it," she says, running her hands down over a dark blue sheath dress that would stun at the Swan.

"Got what?"

"My style. Where are all the cut-off shorts?" She smiles at me, her sparkling eyes dancing, and I go in for a kiss.

After dinner last night, we soaped each other up in the shower in the master bathroom. If nothing else, watching Quinn thoroughly enjoy the simple pleasure of taking a hot shower, the water cascading down over her breasts, revealing her skin from underneath the soap suds, is a memory I'll treasure for the rest of my life.

All day Saturday, I make sure she's pampered to within an inch of her life. I hire the most exclusive masseuse in the area, who brings along a team of two other people to give us a couples massage in the downstairs living area. When Rosemary knocks on my suite's door as we're finishing a five-star breakfast prepared by Robert to tell us they're here, Quinn's eyes light up. "I never get massages anymore," she says, beaming at me. "This place is heaven."

When she's here, it is.

Robert sends us meal after meal of meticulously prepared foods. Even the appetizers are a masterpiece. I wouldn't expect anything less—he's been with our family for a long time, since well before the divorce. I remember my mother sitting poolside, lifting each bite to her lips and then leaning her head back against the plush padding of her lounge chair, closing her eyes while she savored every mouthful.

That's the image that comes to mind when Quinn does the very same thing in her lounge chair by the pool, reflections from the surface of the water dancing across her face, illuminating her exquisite beauty despite the shadows from the oversized sun hat she's wearing. She laughed when she found it in the closet, but she refuses to sit by the pool without it.

Quinn stretches out on a lounge chair again midmorning on

Sunday. The furniture has been replaced at least twice since my parents divorced, but the memory is still so powerful that I can see it right in front of my eyes. A stab of regret spears my heart realizing that Quinn will never get to meet my mother.

Or my brother.

My brother loved this place when we were growing up. The sun always made my head swim after an hour or so, sending me back to my room to read in the relative darkness, but he didn't give a shit—he'd stay out by the pool until the sun set, doing cannonball after cannonball, sending waves of water over the sides of the pool. My father liked to stand at the grill, turning over burger patties and hot dogs—always cooking more than any of us could eat—and transferring them to a ceramic tray with a silver cover.

I was never out there long enough for him, but my brother —he was wild enough to earn my father's affection. A memory surfaces from the depths. A headache blooming behind my eyes, the summer sun too intense, and my father calling after me, "You're like your mother. Too quiet to make any real mark on the world."

Though his tone was mocking and he said the words with a smile, he laughed along with my brother at my retreating back.

I shake it off and fill my eyes, and my mind, with the sight of Quinn, radiant in a slick black bikini, her head tilted back against the cushions of the chair, her perfect body stretched out in total relaxation. I can see the edges of her face underneath the sun hat. Her eyes are closed to shield them against the pool's reflection.

"It's a relief," she says, as if we've been talking this entire time instead of silently enjoying the last morning of the weekend.

"What's a relief?"

"Being free from Derek."

We've been trading life details the entire weekend, but this is the first time she's mentioned him since that night at the apartment. My heart breaks a little that that piece of shit is on her mind, but I can see how the wound would still be fresh.

Secretly, I'm thrilled that she's choosing to open up to me like this. If we can be totally real with each other, then...

I nod, though she still hasn't opened her eyes. "He seems like he was an asshole."

"Somewhere, he still *is* an asshole. I wish I hadn't wasted five years of my life on him."

"Five *years*?"

"The first couple were pretty good. If they hadn't been, I wouldn't have let him move into my house."

"You didn't mention that before."

"That he was living in my house?"

"Yeah."

"It's a little embarrassing to find out that your fiancé has had a woman on the side for an entire year while he's living in your own house. Oh, and that the woman in question is your best friend on top of it."

"Don't be embarrassed," I say, reaching out to rest a hand on her smooth thigh. She gives a soft sigh of satisfaction. "He was a prick who didn't know what he had."

Quinn opens her eyes then and smiles into mine. "Do you know what you have?"

"I have a decent idea." I grin back, my voice husky.

"You know what the worst part was?" she says, lifting her head to kiss the side of my neck, her tongue darting out in a suggestion that we should consider heading back to the bedroom.

"What?"

"The fact that he lied about it for so long." Quinn's gaze turns steely for a moment. "I'm *over* liars." My stomach flops over in a sickening thud.

Then her expression clears, and she's looking at me with a wicked glint in her eyes. "There's something I want to do. We have a little more time before we need to leave, right?"

I'm out of the chair in an instant, offering my hand to her.

"*More* than enough."

33

QUINN

City noise—horns honking, taxi drivers shouting at one another, motorcycles with no mufflers—seems almost oppressive after the luxurious silence at Christian's cottage in the Hamptons.

Cottage. Even thinking about the Pierce Cottage being called that—by anyone, even Christian—still makes me laugh.

As I stand near the outskirts of a SoHo ballroom, watching Christian work the crowd at a fundraiser to raise money for afterschool programs, my mind turns over the memories we created this past weekend. It's been four days since we came back to the city, but my entire soul wants to be back in the perfectly cooled rooms of the mansion, or lounging poolside on the most plush pool furniture I've ever seen in my life.

Christian was relaxed there. Seeing him at the Cottage, away from any prying eyes, was like seeing him at the Bowery Mission at that first event. He was quieter, not so boisterous. I'd half expected him to want to go to summer parties in the evenings to drink and dance with people more of his social class—at least money-wise—but instead he planned evenings in, catered by Robert, for the two of us.

Maybe it's because we can't afford to out ourselves yet.

That's not entirely true. Christian can afford to do anything he wants. I'm the one whose career will come to a crashing halt if anyone finds out I'm dating one of my clients.

My only client, I remind myself sternly. HRM isn't going to look on this relationship very fondly, and that's putting it mildly.

My heart races a little whenever I think about it, but no matter how hard I try, I can't convince myself to break things off with Christian and wait until it's at a better time in my career. Every time I picture telling him to wait, that we need to keep things strictly professional, my soul revolts. A day without touching him, kissing him, talking to him is a wasted day.

I can't do it.

I sigh a little. Since we came back from the Hamptons, I haven't been to Christian's penthouse yet. He's been showing up at Carolyn's in the evenings, sometimes before she goes to bed, and the three of us have a glass of wine and chat. My roommate doesn't seem to have a single qualm about me being with Christian, although this morning, when we were both getting ready to go to work—me at HRM, her at the new boutique—she asked me if I had plans with him after this event.

"I don't know. We might come back here. He might be busy. Why?"

"He seems different."

"Different how?"

Carolyn shrugged. "Not like himself."

At first I felt a flash of anger directed toward my roommate, but the concern in her eyes was genuine. She's known Christian a lot longer than I have.

"Is it something specific?"

Carolyn shook her head. "If I think of what it is, I'll let you know." Then she brightened up. "Maybe he's in love with you and it's making him grow up."

"I hope that's it and it's nothing serious!" I said, grabbing my purse from the hook in the entryway. "You had me a little worried there. If you think of what it is, though, let me know, okay?"

"I will. Have a good day, Q."

Christian finishes shaking hands with a school board member and crosses back across the room to me, a hint of lust hiding behind his polite smile.

"We should get out of here," he says to me quietly. We're both standing up straight, not too close to one another, playing the part of coworkers, colleagues. *Not* a couple.

"Don't even. This is an excellent opportunity. *Tons* of positive press for Pierce Industries." *Jesus*, it takes work to stay professional when he wants to escape.

"I think we both know that positive press is nothing compared to pressing—"

A a booming voice interrupts Christian's naughty comment.

"Pierce!"

We both turn to face a tall man in a dark suit that's tailored perfectly to his towering frame. His freckled face is set off by reddish hair, and he's beaming as he comes in at high speed.

"Matthews!" Christian cries, the very picture of his loud, party-boy self. The two men shake hands, then pound on each other's shoulders.

"How have you been, man?"

Christian holds the guy at arm's length and looks him up and down. "Great, Matthews. *Great*. Where the hell have you been all this time?"

"L.A.," Matthews says, his deep voice rumbling above the chatter of the crowd. "I'm only in town for a month or so—overseeing some new ventures, if you know what I mean."

Christian obviously does know what he means, because he gives Matthews a sage nod.

"Elijah Pierce. What a crazy coincidence to run into you here." My heart stops, but this Matthews guy barrels on. "I'd have thought you'd be some high-class professor by now, or maybe own your own building on campus." Then he pauses and glances around. "Is Chris here anywhere? You guys still go everywhere together, or did he move on?"

Christian's face is white as a ghost, his smile frozen. The corner of his lip jerks and the smile drops away.

Matthews sees it.

"Shit, man. What'd I say?"

Christian sucks in a breath, tries to force another smile onto his face, and almost succeeds. "I hate to tell you this, but Eli—he died about ten years ago."

"Oh, *fuck*," Matthews says, then cups his hands over his mouth. "I'm so sorry. You guys look—you guys looked..." His face flames red. "I had no idea. That must have happened after—"

Christian holds both hands up, waving Matthews' embarrassment away. "Way after you left Dalton."

Matthews is still shaking his head, a hand over his head. "That's terrible. I don't know what to say, Chris."

Christian reaches out and pats his buddy's shoulder in a show of empathy, a genuine smile now back on his face. "No way for you to know, buddy. Listen—give me your number, and we'll meet up again before you leave for L.A. I want to hear all about whatever it is you're wasting your time on over there."

Matthews laughs, his relief palpable, and the two men exchange numbers.

The instant Matthews has receded back into the crowd, Christian spins on his heel to face me, his face wretched with pain.

"That's enough for now."

"Yes," I say gently. "Enough."

"Let's go back to my penthouse."

34

CHRISTIAN

I can't *believe* that happened.

Who the hell would have expected to run into a guy like Greg Matthews at a fundraiser for New York City afterschool shit? Not me. I haven't seen him since the beginning of high school, when his father moved their entire family overseas to start a multinational corporation. He was gone well before my brother died.

On top of that, I can't believe how much this is affecting me.

Hearing those words come out of his mouth has put me into a tailspin, and the fancy food and cocktails served so generously at the beginning of the fundraiser churn in my stomach.

I turn back to face Quinn. She is standing stock-still, her facial expression and posture conveying sympathy.

"That's enough for now."

She can clearly sense how this is non-negotiable because she agrees with me in a soothing tone. "Yes. Enough."

I haven't planned anything for the evening. This week has been packed to the gills, and it's been easier to meet her at her place where there's not a minefield of my personal items to distract us. I told Quinn at the Cottage that I would take her to my penthouse whenever she wanted, but she hasn't brought it up since we came back to the city.

And I've been lying awake at night, trying to figure out what I'm going to do.

I'll tell her.

But how?

How do I open my mouth and reveal this kind of secret to a woman who's had enough lying, cheating behavior to last a lifetime?

Even when I stay at Carolyn's, my arms wrapped snuggly around Quinn, her chest rising and falling against my chest while she breathes, it takes hours for me to fall asleep. As soon as my head hits the pillow, my heart rate skyrockets, beating so hard against my rib cage that I'm surprised it doesn't wake her.

Her words ring in my ears.

I'm over liars.

That's me.

A liar.

If not actively, then at least by omission, which isn't any better.

Now this thing with Matthews.

I'm being driven into a trap, the escape route narrowing and narrowing until it's going to take some kind of bodily sacrifice to get through to the other side.

These thoughts rage in my mind as Louis makes the drive from SoHo to Midtown. Quinn sits silently by my side, holding my hand tightly in hers, and I can't think of a single thing to say. If I open my mouth right now, I might blurt out the awful truth that I've been carrying around with me for ten years.

And now—now is *not* the right time.

Louis pulls up to the curb and hops out, coming around to open Quinn's door. She shades her eyes with her hand and looks up at the building, a skyscraper owned by Pierce Industries.

Calm down, Pierce.

I climb out to stand beside her.

"You're all the way up at the *top*?"

"You've got that right."

I lead her into the building, giving the doorman a nod as we go by.

"Mr. Pierce," he says, nodding back.

"Phillip."

Across from the main bank of elevators is a single shaft that goes one place and one place only: my penthouse. I take the access card out of my breast pocket, where I put it every morning, and swipe it through the reader.

"Highly exclusive," Quinn says as we step inside, and I rub

the small of her back. She's trying to lighten the mood. I let her.

"Only the best," I say lightly, as the car whisks us up, up, up.

When I open the door to the penthouse, Quinn steps inside, her eyes wide and alert. I can tell she's excited, even if she doesn't want to admit it. I wouldn't admit it either, given the scene she witnessed, and the heavy silence that followed us all the way back to the building.

The entryway opens into a massive living area with a wall of windows looking out over the city. As the evening turns to night, and the lights of the buildings start flickering on, it's a breathtaking view.

"Wow," Quinn whispers, walking across to the bank of windows.

"That's not all there is."

I show her the kitchen, the library, the exercise room, and the two guest suites.

"Do you have a chef here, too?"

"I'm thinking of hiring one. Up until recently, I ate at the Swan when I was in the city. I do have a housekeeper, but this place is smaller than the Cottage—she's only here three days a week."

"Smaller? Not by much," Quinn says, as she follows me down the hall to the master suite.

I open the door to reveal a massive king-sized bed, made up with dark sheets and covered by a comforter that looks like it's made out of spun silver.

"Where the action happens," I say, gesturing toward the bed, and Quinn laughs, the sound setting my heart at ease.

"This isn't the only room, is it?" Quinn says.

I roll my eyes. "Of course not."

We walk together, first through the master bedroom, which is easily the size of Quinn's entire room in Carolyn's apartment. Then I take her back across the room and down another hallway, off of which is a den and an office. These rooms are where I spend my time when I'm not at the Swan. I've been here more often recently, missing the hell out of Quinn.

As I watch her run her hands over the books on the shelves in the den, tilting her head to look at the titles, the reality of what I've done—and what it will do to her—tightens around my neck like icy fingers.

Will she ever come here once she knows?

I'll give myself the night with her.

Then I'm going to tell her.

The thing with Matthews—it's thrown my dilemma into stark relief.

I'm over liars.

I need one more night.

35

QUINN

Christian thrusts into me with total abandon like it's his last night on earth—hard, fast, strong, and deep.

I was looking at books in his den. It's an impressive collection, and it distracted me from the silence that fell over the room It distracted me until it didn't. Turning, I dropped my hand.

The words I'd planned to say flew right out of my mind when I saw the look in his eyes.

There was pain there, like he was fighting off something sharp and cruel in his head, but obscuring it was a pure, masculine need. His muscles tensed underneath his jacket. His jaw worked. Then came the smoldering smile that sent electric jolts of lust in a wave from my nipples to the hallowed space between my legs.

I didn't need words to know what to do next.

I crossed the room, pulled him toward me, and kissed him

hard enough to shake the pain loose from where it was stabbing through his heart.

He responded instantly, wrapping his powerful arms around my waist and pulling me in tight, so close to his body that my feet almost left the ground.

It wasn't far from the den to the bed and once he'd carried me there, we attacked each other's clothes until they were all piled in a rumpled heap on the floor.

He pushed me down onto my back on the bed and I arched up to meet him, locking my arms around his neck, kissing him even deeper, and then I shoved my weight upward and sideways, turning us over by sheer force of will.

I straddled him, bucking against his hardness, already slick, the wetness coating his skin.

"Jesus," he said on an exhale, the heat of the word catching in the hollow of my shoulder.

I took that as a sign to press into him more forcefully, striking a rhythm, drawing my wetness over his shaft again and again until I felt his muscles clenching underneath me, his hips rising to meet mine with more intensity. Then, in one smooth movement, I lined myself up over his cock and drove my hips down toward his, taking him all in.

When our bodies slammed together, he heaved a guttural sound from behind clenched teeth that was half relief, half desperation. It unlocked something in me, pushing me over the edge to wildness, and I worked against him with a fury I had never before experienced in my life.

It took him by surprise. I could tell by the sharp breath he drew in, but it only took him seconds to parallel my pace and intensity, taking in everything I had to give him, hands pressed tightly on my hips to pull me down onto him even harder than I could manage by myself.

Next thing I know, he's lifting me away from him, turning me, so that I'm on hands and knees, my palms pressed into the million-thread-count comforter beneath me. Christian positions himself behind me, lines the head of his cock up with my opening, and stops. I'm panting breathlessly.

It's a cruel tease.

I buck my hips backward against him, trying to get him to sink inside me, but he resists. His hands are clenched on my hips, gripping tightly and steadily, like he wants to be in control.

I can give him that.

I press my breasts down against the comforter and arch my back, head down, ass up, hands clenching the comforter. "Fuck me." I know he wants to hear it as much as I want to say it.

"Beg."

His voice is hard, uncompromising, and the tone sends a new gush of wetness between my legs.

"Please!" I urge. "*Please.*"

He remains still for three more heartbeats and I clutch the comforter in my fists, willing myself to stay down, to stay still. He is *loving* this. Something about that man's mistake at the fundraiser made him feel out of control—that much is clear—and though I can't read his mind, I'd bet my life savings that this is exactly the remedy he needs.

Is that all this is? says the little voice in my head, but it's struck down by the rest of my body, which is dying to have him inside me again.

This is *who he is*, the one behind all the barriers put up in public, behind all the social constrictions, behind closed doors.

With me and me alone.

It's a great deal, if he would—

At that moment he crashes into me with such a powerful thrust that it takes my breath away, crushes my chest into the bed, makes my pussy clench around Christian's steely hardness. I'm moments away from climax, and I squeeze my eyes shut, gasp in a breath. My body responds to him, going higher, higher, *higher* until I'm careening over, crying out into the mattress. Moments later I hear Christian's answering roar as he pins me back against him and comes hard, his hips spasming even as he stays buried deep inside me.

We're frozen in that position for a heartbeat, then two, and then he pulls out and falls forward onto the bed, maneuvering up to the pillows while he turns me over onto my side with one hand, his arm wrapped around my waist.

He doesn't say anything.

It's not long before his breathing steadies and slows.

I lay there next to him, his breathing steady. The room darkens as the sun sets behind the buildings. My mind is too hyped up to sleep, too caught up in the electrifying encounter we had.

When I can't stand it any longer, I gently disengage his arm from my waist and slip out of bed. I don't want to put on my outfit from the office—a sleeveless dress and a short-sleeved blazer—but I don't have any other clothes with me, so my first stop is Christian's walk-in closet. In one of the lower drawers, I find a pair of lounge pants and a plain t-shirt that smell like him. I throw it on, luxuriating in the softness of the cloth.

I don't want to look at my phone in the dark room and risk waking him up, so I pad down the hall to his den, with its bookshelves and leather furniture. There's a certain armchair I'm dying to sink into.

There's a small table lamp in the corner that gives the room a pleasing glow. I shut the door closed behind me. The armchair, tucked in the corner and surrounded by shelves full of first editions and other of Christian's favorites, is both plushly soft and supportive. I curl up in it, tucking my legs underneath me in a comfortable and relaxing position, and sigh. Pure satisfaction.

I'm about to unlock the screen of my phone when something on a nearby shelf catches my eye. It's a journal like the other ones I saw at the Cottage—exactly the same, but it's all by itself.

I bite my lip. I shouldn't snoop. Absolutely not.

If I do, I can admit it to him later on.

It's probably an archive of teenage angst in written form.

I pull the journal down from the shelf and start to flip through it.

There are pages and pages of neat handwriting, so neat that

it makes me want to put it back. This kind of writing doesn't seem like it would be something the party animal Christian that I know would write, and suddenly I'm struck by my actions, and what a terrible invasion of privacy this is.

I turn the journal over in my hands to close it, but my nail catches on the back cover, revealing the very last page.

There, scratched in a panicked scrawl, the writing appearing so different from that which has been written throughout the rest of the book, are words that make my heart thud with anxious fear.

WHAT HAVE I DONE

I HAVE TO BE HIM

FOREVER

FOREVER

FOREVER

My stomach lurches and churns as my mind spins into overdrive. This is some kind of joke, right? Or some kind of teenage outburst? The hairs prickling up on the back of my neck tell me I'm wrong. This is something I was never supposed to see. Something *nobody* was ever supposed to see.

I'm flashing back, reflecting and piecing together one memory after the other, of all the things I've seen Christian do since we met on that rainy day on the sidewalk. Then I remember the way he froze up when I asked about memorials during our very first meeting. The way it pissed him off when I said he was like a different person at the Bowery Mission. The way his face went white as a ghost when that man, Matthews, called him by his brother's name.

His brother's name.

Elijah.

Then the final piece clicks into place, and I clap my own hand over my mouth to keep from screaming.

Christian's tattoo.

My eyes lingered on it that afternoon at the Cottage, tracing the lines, trying to make sense of each of the sections.

Carolyn's voice haunts my thoughts. *They got matching tattoos the same week that he died.*

In one of those sections of the tattoos, between the silhouettes of various predatory animals, is an intricate design. If you look at it for long enough, it resolves into a letter.

But the letter on Christian's chest isn't a C.

It's an E.

36

CHRISTIAN

When I wake up, I instinctively reach for Quinn.

The spot in the bed next to me is empty.

Groggily, I sit up and rub at my eyes. What that hell? What time is it? Did I pass out that hard after we had sex?

The only light evident in the room is the ambient glow of New York City's lights. It's late.

Did she leave?

I stretch my arms over my head, working out the kinks, then throw my legs over the side of the bed.

Now that my eyes have adjusted, I can see that there's some light escaping from the door to the den, and a smile plays across my face. She's probably in there with her head tilted to the side, reading all the book titles. Picturing it makes my chest warm. Quinn doesn't talk about books much, but the respectful way she touches them tells me that when the mood strikes her, she loves to find a good one and disappear inside its pages.

First things first. I move quickly to the walk-in closet and pull a fresh pair of boxers and a t-shirt from a drawer, sliding them up and on, tugging the shirt over my head. I'm sure we'll be going back to bed shortly, but in case Quinn isn't in the mood for more sex—

I laugh softly to myself. If I know her—and after the time we've spent together lately, I think I know her pretty well—she'll be in the mood as soon as she sees me walk through the door.

I brush my teeth in the master bathroom, then flick off the light and head back down toward the den.

Pausing outside the door, I listen for any sound of movement inside. It doesn't seem like she's moving around or about to open the door. My heart rate picks up. Ever since my brother died, it makes me nervous to go into a silent room at night.

But I'm not going to stand out here forever, wondering what's going on inside my own den.

It's my girlfriend, likely reading a book, maybe fast asleep in one of my plush as hell armchairs.

I swing the door open.

There's Quinn, in the armchair, her hand over her mouth, her eyes wide and horrified, locked on me, frozen.

She's holding the one and only journal I kept in this house on her lap, and it's open to the very last page.

The photo of my brother and me stares at me from where

it's positioned on the shelf behind her head, nestled amongst a collection of Hardy Boys books that my mother bought us. In it, our arms are thrown around each other and we're laughing in the city sun. It was taken the week he died.

She knows.

My heart plummets. It's like an icy knife has slipped down the length of my spine; it's painful and sickening all at once.

"What—" The word comes out as a croaking whisper. I try again. "What are you doing?"

Quinn's hand falls from her mouth, but the expression on her face doesn't change at all. "Tell me this is some crazy teenage bullshit that you wrote when you were having a bad day ten years ago."

Her voice is sharp and cold, and I know that she's using everything in her power to protect herself from me in this moment. I want so badly to lie to her, to reassure her that *of course* it's the ramblings of a dumbass teenage kid, some idiotic nonsense that you scrawl late at night when you're drunk and rich and stupid.

But I can't.

Because it's not.

I take in a shaky breath and open my mouth to tell her the truth, but I can't force the words out.

She sees it in my eyes.

"What the hell does this mean?" she says, standing. She thrusts the journal at me so I can read the words on the page. I don't need to read them. I know them by heart. Then she throws it back into the chair. "What does it *mean*?"

"I—"

The words stick in my throat. This is not how I wanted this to play out. This is not how I wanted her to discover the worst thing I've done, the secret that I've been keeping from everyone for the past ten years of my life.

Quinn narrows her eyes, straightens her back, and crosses her arms over her chest.

Steps toward me.

Her voice is soft, deadly.

"Let me see your tattoo."

My heart is in my throat. It's going to burst out and splatter all over the ground.

This is it.

This is *it*.

I reach up and grab the collar of my t-shirt in one of my fists, then yank it down so that my tattoo is visible.

Her eyes go instantly to it, and she steps forward another few inches.

She looks harder.

Her eyes dart to my face.

Back at the tattoo.

Then she reaches out with one finger and traces the E hidden in the design with her fingernail.

"E. For Elijah."

Her voice is soft, but it carries a punch of disappointment that almost brings me to my knees.

Then she jerks back, putting several feet between us, her eyes horrified again.

"*Why*?"

I'm back in that bedroom again, kneeling by my brother's lifeless body, consumed with the knowledge that I will live the rest of my days with my father's disapproval. Every time he looks at me, he will wish my brother was still alive. He would rather have his infectious energy in his life than my unassuming presence. And so, before I dial 9-1-1, before I summon the police, before I break down in front of them, screaming, sobbing, pleading—I take my brother's wallet from his pocket, and I replace it with my own.

"I couldn't—I couldn't face it," I say, my voice strangled from the pain. "He was my father's favorite. I couldn't be the one to keep living with that. So when the cops came—my dad was out of the country, he didn't even show up for another twenty-four hours—I said I was him. It was easy to switch our I.D.s. We'd never been fingerprinted. We were identical twins. No one could ever tell us apart. Nobody ever—nobody ever questioned me."

"What the *fuck*," Quinn says, shaking her head. "Who *are* you?"

The question hangs in the air between us, and I give her the only answer I can think to give.

"Elijah Pierce."

She puts both of her hands up, palms toward me, and lets

out a sharp breath. "I don't even want to know why. I don't even want to know."

Then she reaches behind her, snatches her phone from the chair, and looks at me one last time.

"We're over...*Elijah*."

Quinn shoves past me and hurries out into the dark hallway.

There is a faint rustling as she collects her clothes, and then I hear her running footsteps as she makes her way to the bedroom door and flees.

She's gone from this part of my life.

Forever.

37

QUINN

Oh, my God.

Oh, my God.

Oh my *God*.

What *happened*?

Mind reeling, I run back to Christian's bedroom and scoop up my clothes and shoes into my arms. My heart is in my throat and my breath ragged, and not in a fun, sexy way, but in a terrified, get-me-away-from-this-psycho way.

Who have I been sleeping with?

Not Christian Pierce.

His reactions keep tumbling over and over in my mind, all of them suddenly clicking into place like a child's puzzle, so easy once you have all the pieces.

Holy *shit*.

I knew there were things he didn't like to talk about, his

brother being first on the list. I knew that certain things people said set him off, even if they seemed innocuous. I never imagined that he was hiding something of this magnitude.

You did imagine it.

The elevator seems to be descending in slow motion to the lobby. I'm so panicked that I don't care about my outfit—being dressed in Christian's too-large lounge clothes is the least of my worries right now.

The voice in the back of my mind is right.

There was a moment, back in the car, when I thought there was something beneath the surface of Christian's mood, his movements, his expressions, but it was so fleeting that I forgot about it until right now.

I cannot forget what I saw in the journal.

I will never be able to forgive what Christian told me he had done.

No—that's not right. If he wants to do some fucked-up shit like pretend to be his dead twin brother for ten years, that's his business. But *keeping* it from me? Keeping secrets from the woman you're supposed to love? And not *any* secret, but *this* secret?

How could he tell you?

There's no time to think about this right now, no time to process it.

The elevator dings that it has arrived at the ground floor and the doors slide open. For an instant, I'm seized by a wild fear that Christian has somehow beaten me down here and is waiting for me in the lobby, and my legs freeze up.

Go!

Sucking in a deep breath, I force myself to move.

As soon as I'm outside the elevator, I lock my gaze on the front doors, too petrified to look left or right, too terrified to see if he's following me.

Don't be such a pansy, Quinn, I think to myself, and as I jog toward the entrance in my bare feet, I whip my head around.

The rest of the lobby is empty, silent, except for, "Ma'am?"

The doorman's voice rings out and echoes against the wall, the sound bombarding my ears.

"What?" I shout, my voice too loud, my eyes wild, as I spin around to face him. Where can I go? I can't stay here.

"Are you all right?"

"No. I need to go. I need to *go*."

"Would you like for me to call you a cab?"

I scan the lobby one more time, then glance out the glass doors at the front of the building. No cabs are waiting—not a surprise this late at night. I make a split-second decision. The doorman at a building like this will be able to get someone here faster than I can on my own.

"Call a cab and tell them to get here as soon as they can. I'll be waiting outside."

"You're more than welcome to wait in here."

I clench my teeth. "Please call. I'll be outside."

He nods calmly in the face of my desperation, then picks up the phone. I don't wait to hear what he says. I move, press my hands against the smooth metal strip in the center of the door to push it open, and walk out into the summer heat.

My first instinct is to run, but now that I'm outside, cars trundling slowly by on the streets, I don't want to draw attention to myself. Instead, I walk calmly away from the doors and press my back up against the warm stone wall of the building.

My hands are shaking, and my grip on the disorganized collection of clothes and purse in my hands is so tight my knuckles are white. It takes a conscious effort to relax, but as soon as I do, my teeth start chattering, even though the air is thick with humid heat rising from the pavement.

I want to call Carolyn, anyone, but my phone is buried somewhere in my clothes, and I know digging for it now will cause the whole thing to fall all over the sidewalk. Not worth the risk, especially if Christian comes out after me.

The thought sends a new spike of adrenaline streaking through my veins.

Am I making myself a sitting duck, standing out here alone like this?

Is it any worse than walking through the streets of New York in the middle of the night, looking bedraggled and paranoid?

If Christian—Elijah?—would lie about who he is, what else would he lie about?

I don't know *anything* about what happened ten years ago.

A fresh horror dawns. What if he didn't steal his brother's identity when his twin died of an overdose? What if he murdered him?

The bile rises in my throat, and I swallow hard, willing myself not to throw up.

There are too many questions, not enough answers, and a raw, searing pain. I was taken for a fool.

Again.

Somehow, this is far worse than what Derek did to me. How much worse, I'm still not sure.

Have I been secretly dating a murderer?

What do I do *now*?

Not only dating and having the best sex of my life with him, I remind myself with a churning gut. *Working* for him. Working *with* him. Making him seem so trustworthy, so responsible...

It's the early hours of Friday morning *right now*. I have about five hours before I need to be back in the HRM offices. I'm drawing a complete blank on whether I have any meetings scheduled with Christian today—I can't think of him by any other name, I *can't* right now. How can I sit across from him in a meeting? A cold sweat trickles down the back of my neck even though it's hotter than sin out here.

I'll call in sick. That's what I'll do.

A yellow cab turns the corner. I peer through the windshield, another sickening anxiety gripping me—what if it's the same driver from the airport? I don't think I'll be able to take it.

But it's not him.

It's a young man with dark hair and he appears reserved and quiet, and relief sweeps over me as I slide across the cracked leather seat and pull the door closed behind me.

Clearing my throat, I rattle off my address.

As he pulls the car away from the curb, I crane my neck to look behind us, half expecting to see Christian run out onto the sidewalk.

For a moment, I'm disappointed.

"Jesus Christ," I whisper to myself, sinking back into the seat as the cab carries me forward into the first part of my escape from the man I thought I loved.

38

CHRISTIAN

The thing about your worst nightmares?

They always come true.

39

QUINN

It's easy to sound sick on the phone when I call the HRM offices and leave a message that I won't be in. It's like I've been run over by a Mack truck. My stomach hasn't unknotted itself since I left Christian's apartment, and my mind is scattered in pieces, not to mention my heart.

Carolyn knocks on my bedroom door Friday morning on her way out to the boutique. "Hey," she calls out softly. "Can I come in?"

I grumble something unintelligible from beneath my cocoon of covers. The door swings open, and seconds later the bed dips as Carolyn's weight presses down on the mattress.

"Are you the only one?"

I poke my head out from underneath the comforter. What the hell is she talking about?

"The only one what?"

My roommate gestures at my state of being. "This looks like a pretty nasty bug. Is it taking over the office, or are you the only one who got it? I think the subways are giant germ incubators."

I roll away from her with a groan.

She was asleep when I came back last night, so I didn't have to tell her what happened.

I could lie about it, but that would make me a massive hypocrite.

My stomach turns over. I can't tell her the whole truth.

I don't think I can say those words out loud.

Part of me wants to, but speaking them out loud to her might cause me to actually vomit all over the sheets...and Carolyn.

"It's not a bug."

I feel Carolyn's movement rather than see it—the straightening of her back. "Q, did something happen at work?"

"Not at work, no." In spite of myself, a painful lump rises in my throat, and tears prick at the corner of my eyes, threatening to spill out and down my cheeks. Without turning to face her, I choke out what little of the truth I can manage. "Christian and I—we're over."

"Oh, *no*," she says, and I can hear the sympathy in her voice. "I'm so sorry, Quinn. I thought—" Her sentence trails off, and she reaches out to pat my shoulder. "I know how excited you were to be with him. That's awful."

Pressing my lips into a thin line, I swallow the tightness in my throat and roll over onto my back. "It's probably for the best."

Carolyn's face is a mask of concern. "Do you want me to stay with you today? We could go shopping, have lunch—take your mind off things."

I shake my head. "It's pathetic, I know, but I think I need a day to...process everything."

That couldn't be more true.

"Okay," she says, standing up. "If you get hungry, order from wherever you want. It's on me. I've got running tabs everywhere in the city." I give her a small smile. Carolyn is a good friend. If nothing else, I have that. "And there's ice cream in the freezer. Help yourself."

"I will."

Carolyn wags a finger at me. "You're not spending the entire weekend in bed, though. Not even over a guy like Christian Pierce. We're going to have fun. At least, *I'm* going to have fun. All you have to do is come with me."

It makes me laugh, and my heart lightens a little. "It's a deal.

I spend the rest of the day parked on the couch. At first my heart is numb and then it's throbbing, alternating every minute.

I don't know what to think.

My initial terror has subsided, at least a little. Maybe I don't know what the hell I'm talking about, but if Christian was some kind of serial murderer and had it in for me, I'd be dead by now.

On top of that, a suspicious death like that would have been investigated. Especially for someone like him. If there had been any hint of foul play, Carolyn would have told me about it. There's no way she would have let me get involved with a potentially dangerous person, even if they had been friends since they were in boarding school.

There's no way she would remain friends with a murderer. I'm sure of that.

It still doesn't explain why he stole his brother's identity.

Even if he did it in a moment of grief—why keep up the facade for another ten years?

Something else is going on with him.

I don't want anything to do with it.

That's a lie.

My heart collapses again, and tears come to my eyes. The awful truth is that I miss Christian. I felt alive when I was with him, complete in a way that I hadn't since I found out what Derek was doing.

That whole thing threw me for a loop.

I didn't deserve to be cheated on. I was attentive and funny and supportive and all the things a fiancée is supposed to be.

"Ugh," I groan to the empty room. That's not the point. Derek should have been honest, even if he wasn't happy with the way I was.

Christian should have been honest, too.

But it's not only me he's been lying to.

That's the scariest part about this. He's been fooling everyone—his father, his friends—for a decade, and for what?

I can't figure it out.

I want to pick up my phone right now and call him, demanding to know why the hell he did what he did. He could have at least told me, a woman he claimed to love. A woman he claimed to love after ten years of refusing to date anyone seriously.

What would you have done then?

Exactly what you did.

Jesus, the truth hurts.

There's no good way to admit to another person that you've been living a lie for ten years. When you lie about something that fundamental it colors everything else. What wouldn't he lie about if he would lie about his own identity?

Did he love me?

A sob catches in my throat. I can't be certain, but I felt it, and I thought it was real.

I know with certainty it was—it *is*—real for me.

Can I help it that part of me wants him back?

40

CHRISTIAN

"Mr. Pierce?"

I'm rousing from the black, peaceful depths of alcohol-induced sleep, and the voice sounds like it's coming from underwater.

No. I don't want to wake up.

All I want is to go back in time, destroy that journal, and keep Quinn in bed with me all night, for the rest of my life.

I bury my head back under the pillow and squeeze my eyes shut.

The knock comes again.

"Mr. Pierce?"

With an exasperated sigh, I throw the covers off my body and lurch to the side, swinging my legs over the edge of the bed and planting my feet on the floor.

That was a mistake.

My stomach lurches with the movement, and now that I'm upright, the full extent of my hangover is readily apparent.

I bury my face in my hands, my palms meeting the rough stubble there.

I haven't shaved since last Thursday.

I feel like shit.

The air in the room is stale and close, and the drinking and lack of showering hasn't done anything to improve it.

Another knock at my bedroom door.

"Mr. Pierce..." It's Sarah, my city housekeeper. Her voice sounds concerned, urgent.

"One second," I snap back, my tone harsh, and then I stand up, my legs wobbling underneath me.

Somewhere in this mess is a t-shirt. I find it crumpled near the head of the bed and put it on, not bothering to cover my boxers with pants. It's Sarah out there, not the Queen of England.

By the time I get to the door that leads to the rest of the penthouse, my head feels like there are jagged spikes being driven into it from every angle.

This is not a very promising start to the day.

Whatever day it is.

Yanking the door open, I reveal myself—and am instantly blinded by the light streaming in from the hallway.

"*Shit*," I cry, throwing a hand up over my eyes. "Can you turn that off?"

There are muted footsteps as Sarah retreats down the hall, and then I hear the click of the switch being flipped. Behind my palm, the hallway darkens. I lower my hand and watch Sarah come back down the hallway, her round frame broken up by a crisp white apron.

She tilts her head back to look at my face, then purses her lips.

"You need to get out of that bedroom, Mr. Pierce."

I roll my eyes, a movement I regret immediately. It throws me off-balance and sends another bolt of pain through my head. "Go away, Sarah."

Sarah has raised six children, so she's not about to take my foul attitude at face value. Her no-bullshit demeanor is why I hired her to come around three days a week.

"Unlikely," she replies, pushing her way past me and into the bedroom. Seconds later, the space is flooded with sunlight as she snaps open the shades and flicks on a lamp in the corner. "This room is filthy, and you've been wallowing in it for two days."

"How do you know?"

She gives me a look like I'm an idiot, then begins picking up the clothes strewn across the carpet. "I came Friday. Do you remember?"

I narrow my eyes, trying to recall any detail about Friday. What comes to mind is Quinn.

We had a meeting scheduled for 10:00 that morning. Once she left, running out of my apartment like I was a serial killer, I stayed up the rest of the night, alternating between devastation and terror.

What if Quinn went back to her apartment and told Carolyn everything?

What if she told Pierce Industries everything?

Those thoughts were incessant, unyielding. As soon as I convinced myself that she wouldn't—Carolyn wouldn't believe her over me, and of course my *father* wouldn't—the whole damn circus would start over.

Why did I expect a different reaction from her?

Why did I ever think that what we felt for each other—that powerful, wild current running between us—would override a lie of that magnitude?

For the rest of the night, there was nothing to do but wait.

Finally, I decided to proceed as if nothing had happened. We could work things out at the meeting, in a relatively neutral location.

I showered and dressed, chose my favorite suit—a charcoal summer-weight piece made in Italy—and had Louis take me to the Pierce Industries building.

In the office I was my usual charming, slightly cutting self, joking with the secretaries, sitting through update meetings, but I was burning up inside the entire time, the life bleeding out of me with every memory of Quinn's hatred, her terror.

At 9:30, I'd texted Louis to bring the car around to head to her office for our meeting when my office phone rang.

"Christian Pierce."

"Hello, Mr. Pierce. I'm calling from Ms. Campbell's office. Unfortunately, she's no longer available for your meeting this morning."

Disappointment floods my chest. "Did she give a reason?" I said into the receiver, my voice hitching enough to be embarrassing.

The guy on the other end of the line didn't mention it if he noticed anything. "She called in sick early this morning, sir. I see from her schedule you have another meeting next Wednesday. Would you like me to reschedule for Monday?"

"No," I said sharply, then reminded myself that none of this was the assistant's fault.

It was mine.

"No. That's all right." It was hard to force the words out past the lump in my throat.

I hung up, pushed back from my desk, and snatched my phone off its surface. And then I was moving without thinking, through the office, down to the lobby, and out the door. The town car idled at the curb, and I got in.

"HRM?" Louis called from the front.

"The penthouse. Now."

It didn't take me long to get absolutely wasted that day.

"No, Sarah. I don't remember you being here Friday."

"You wouldn't let me in. You were in quite the state, from what I could gather." She puts a hand on her hip and cocks it to the side. "Get into the shower, Mr. Pierce. It's almost noon. Time to go to work."

41

QUINN

Carolyn didn't give me a spare moment to wallow all weekend. A silver lining, at least. And my insurance company called to tell me that the check for my burned-down house would be disbursed in thirty days or less.

Those two things mean that when I arrive at the office on Monday, I'm not a complete wreck.

My heart is hollow, wasted, empty, but my mind is clear—well, clearer, at least.

I'll do this job for long enough to get out of it.

Adam is already at his desk when I stride past, head held high. Nobody is going to know that I got involved with my client. Nobody is going to know that he shattered my heart into a thousand tiny shards and left it there for me to sweep up.

The only saving grace is that I don't have a meeting scheduled with him today.

The next few weeks are going to hurt like a motherfucker.

This is exactly why you don't date clients, I think, settling into the chair behind my desk and wading into a million reminders about Christian and his lies. His name is on every document and my computer is filled with press pictures.

I spend the morning sending bright and chipper responses to charity after charity, shoving my heartbreak deep down where it can't touch me.

It works...for a while.

By noon, I'm trying to tread water while waves of turmoil suck me under the surface.

Thank God for Carolyn.

I switch off my computer screen and breeze out past Adam. "I've got a lunch date," I say to him with as much of a smile as I can force onto my face. "Be back in an hour."

Carolyn meets me at a hole-in-the-wall Thai place halfway between the HRM offices and her boutique. The service is lightning fast. It seems like the waiter brings the food out as soon as we've handed back the menus. Normally, that kind of speed would be cause for suspicion—can a kitchen at *any* restaurant cook *anything* that fast?—but I'm so desperate to unload some of this heaviness from my heart and soul that I don't care. I dig in.

"What's on your mind, Q?" Carolyn says between bites. I haven't said a word about Christian yet. I thought I was playing it cooler than that.

Guess not.

I search for the words as I swallow a bite of pork noodles.

"I'm not over him." My voice comes out low and strained, and Carolyn frowns.

"It's only been a few days. Give yourself time."

The feelings I've been struggling to keep at bay all morning crash through me again.

How can I be so conflicted?

What Christian did—is still doing—is unforgivable.

I open my mouth to tell Carolyn what he did, what he revealed to me last week, but I choke on the words.

Even though he's in the wrong, and even though I'm furious with him, I can't bring myself to betray him.

Not entirely.

I close my mouth again and shake my head, then I lift another bite to my lips. It turns to tasteless mush in my mouth. I force myself to swallow anyway.

Carolyn puts down her fork and leans back in her chair. "What happened between you two?" She gives me a hard look, and I wait for her to put her hands in the air between us, to tell me that we don't have to talk about this.

She doesn't.

"He—he admitted something to me that is unforgivable, so I left. I turned my back on him and left."

I expect Carolyn to look confused, but instead her eyes narrow, and she looks to the side, her jaw working. "So he cheated on you. *God*, what an asshole. That is so *typical*—"

It would be so convenient to let her believe it. It would be an answer everyone would accept, expect even, but I can't let it lie. I cut her off.

"He didn't cheat on me."

Now confusion *does* settle in over her features. "Then what was it?"

This is my opening, my big chance. But I'm looking across the table at Carolyn, who has known Christian since they were teenagers. She was among his closest friends in school. If she doesn't know already, it's not my place to tell her.

"I can't tell you, Care."

She looks a little pissed off with *me* now.

"Seriously, Q? I've known him for years. What are you going to tell me that I don't already know?"

I shake my head. "I can't tell you. Please. Trust me on this."

She sighs. "Fine. But Q—" she leans forward again, into the table, and picks up her fork. "You're a mess. You had a blank look in your eyes all weekend, and now you look like you're about to cry."

As soon as she says it, a tear wells up in one of my eyes and squeezes out onto my eyelashes.

No. I am *done* crying over men. I wasted enough tears on Derek, that scumbag.

I snatch up my napkin and carefully collect the tear, then flatten the paper back over my lap.

"I'm not going to cry over him. Not anymore, Care."

"Okay," she says softly. She searches my face for the truth behind the words, then she looks back down at her plate.

We eat in silence for a little while longer.

"Could you blame me if I did, though?" I finally choke out. Carolyn is my best friend in the city—maybe the entire country, at this point.

"No," she says, "I wouldn't blame you." When she looks at me again, her expression is a mix of concern and curiosity. "But Q—was it something you can't look past? I know Christian is a player, but underneath all the womanizing and partying and the cocky attitude, he's—" She pauses, biting at her lip. "I thought he was a good guy."

Her words crack something open inside me, and then she lands the final blow.

"I've never seen anyone so excited to be with another person as you were about him, Q. If you're ready for it to be over, then I respect that decision. But if you're not? If you're not convinced you can spend the rest of your life without him? Maybe he's worth a second chance."

42

CHRISTIAN

My father summons me to his office as soon as I arrive at Pierce Industries.

On the way up, I try to look like nothing is wrong, like my tardiness is a result of a weekend-long bender. It should be easy enough to explain. I haven't been at the Swan much in the past few weeks, but who cares? I certainly haven't been shutting down the place like I used to.

His secretary makes me wait, which is a sure sign that he's irritated about something. When he finally comes out from behind his door to wave me back nearly ten minutes later, I've almost stopped caring. If I stop moving, even for a second, I'm flooded with thoughts of Quinn.

She's the only thing that matters to me, even if she's gone.

My father walks back around to his seat behind his desk and sits down, glancing at his computer screen. I follow his lead, taking my seat across from him in front of the desk, and wait while he clicks at something.

The silence lasts for a long thirty seconds.

Then he turns away from the computer, crosses his arms in front of him, and speaks.

"It's a bad habit to get into, son."

I raise my eyebrows at him. "Which habit are we talking about?"

"Strolling into the office halfway through the afternoon."

I cross my own arms over my chest and nod. "It's not a habit until you've done it twice."

"Remember that the next time you're tempted to sleep late."

My father says this neutrally, with no hint of mockery.

Then the corners of his mouth turn up, and his eyes glint in the light coming through his windows. "It must have been one hell of a party."

I return his smile automatically, and the lie comes easily to my lips.

"Can't argue with that."

"Listen," he says, uncrossing his arms. "I'm impressed with the work HRM is doing for you. Who did they assign the account to? I'd like to send him my thanks."

My throat tightens, and I cover my mouth with my hand, pretending to cough while I swallow painfully. "It's a she, actually. Quinn Campbell."

"Quinn Campbell," my father says thoughtfully, testing her name in his mouth.

I wish I were telling him the name of the woman I was planning to spend the rest of my life with. I want him to be saying her name, then asking me more about her. I want him to say her name again when I introduce the two of them, and having him shake my hand, congratulating me on finding the perfect woman, a woman far too good for me, a woman I will never regret marrying.

Instead, he's saying the name of the woman who is going to be forced to work with me for the foreseeable future even though my despicable behavior has destroyed any chance of me ever being with her.

"The woman deserves a raise," he says finally, slapping a hand down on the surface of his desk.

It's a struggle to keep the smile on my face. "She does."

My father considers me. "It's not all her, though, is it?"

"I don't know what you're talking about." My tone is light, almost teasing, but I honestly have no idea what he's referring to.

"Not one person has come to my office to tell me that you've been in the tabloids in, what, three weeks? That's unheard of, Chris."

I shrug. "Needed a break."

"You sure that's it?" My father gives me a conspiratorial grin. "It seems awfully sudden for you to drop out of the scene."

"What do you know about the scene?" I say, rolling my eyes, even though my heart is pounding so hard against my rib cage that I'm surprised it doesn't burst out and fall to the floor.

"Nothing," he says, his eyes still twinkling. "I thought maybe there was a woman involved."

My half smile isn't genuine, but he seems not to notice. "I'm always involved with a woman, one way or another."

He gives me a chuckle. "You're like me. Well, the way I was, in my younger days." As he says it, something flashes in his eyes for a split second—too quickly for me to pinpoint the expression. "Never mind all that. I thought the sudden absence from the gossip pages meant you had someone a little more...permanent in your life."

This conversation is killing me. Of course I had someone more permanent in mind. What other reason could I have for making such an abrupt change to the identity I've been cultivating for a full decade? Only love...

The thought brings me up short, but I can't let myself off the hook. Not this time.

Only love would bring a man to that conclusion.

Real love, raw love, the kind of love that strips away all the bullshit from your life, even if you don't want it to, even if you're begging for it not to.

I loved Quinn like that.

I *love* Quinn like that.

I'll never *stop* loving Quinn like that.

I know that now.

"When I find a woman who will keep me out of the gossip sites, you'll be...among the first fifty people to know," I say, keeping my tone light through enormous effort. This meeting *has* to end soon, because there are things I need to figure out.

Things I need to do.

I stand up from the chair and smooth out my jacket, giving my father a grin that matches his. This time, it almost feels real.

At the door, I pause a moment and turn back to address my father.

"I know it's a bad habit," I say jauntily, with the kind of attitude I know my father loved from the real Christian, "but I'm going to lean into it today. There's something I need to do. Don't rat me out to management, okay?"

My father shakes his head, his smile giving him away. With one hand he waves me out of the office. As I turn away, I hear him say one more thing, "That's my boy."

43

QUINN

I still haven't made up my mind about Christian.

And it's *Wednesday.*

I keep working myself up into the strongest frenzied conviction that the lying asshole deserves no part of my life, blinking any stray tears from my eyes, and throwing myself into whatever I'm doing—planning Christian's events for the next month, watching *Bridesmaids* with Carolyn, running on the treadmill at the gym. I wasn't going to buy a membership in the city, but yesterday when I got out of work, I was ready to burst from all the excess nervous energy that had built up from an entire day of looking at Christian's name over and over again. I'd have preferred to run along the sidewalks, but when I stepped outside the HRM offices, the hundred-plus-degree heat hit me like a brick wall. So I did what any desperate person would do: I went to the Midtown Nike store, bought myself an exercise outfit and athletic shoes, and looked up the closest gym to my apartment on Google. A day pass was forty dollars, but I didn't care. I needed to run.

I ran on the treadmill until my lungs burned in my chest, until my legs felt weak and my knees like jelly. At home, I found my roommate already parked on the sofa. Carolyn had called it an early day at the boutique. Once I was out of the shower, I flopped down onto the couch next to her, and we both stretched our legs out, our feet propped up on the ottoman.

"Another rough day?"

I rolled my eyes and sighed deeply.

"Every day is a rough day when your only client is your ex-boyfriend."

"I bet. *Trainwreck* is on HBO. Want to order in?"

"More than anything."

By the end of that movie, I'd changed my mind about Christian again. So he did a terrible thing. Who hasn't made a mistake? Casting the first stone, and all that.

Of course, not *everyone* steals their dead brother's identity and goes on pretending to be him for another ten years, tricking his friends and remaining family the entire time.

I'm exhausted. I woke up like this. It's as if I haven't slept.

There's a meeting with Christian scheduled for 10:00.

I'm torn.

On the one hand, my stomach is twisting in painful knots at the prospect of sitting across my desk from Christian and pretending I feel nothing. I could curl up under the comforter and stay in bed all day, avoiding the scene entirely. It's tempting.

On the other hand, I haven't seen him since last Thursday... and it's killing me. I'm so angry at him. I'm so baffled by what he chose to do. But something deep inside me wants to be close to him, wants to be touching him, wants to be *fighting* with him even, if that's what it takes to get past this.

I shove the covers away and get out of bed in a huff. I need to make up my mind.

I turn on the shower, adjusting the water to the perfect temperature, and step inside.

More than anything, I need to be a professional. HRM was my ticket out of Colorado, and if nothing else, it can be my ticket away from Christian, too.

I stop mid-shampoo. That solution doesn't sit right, either. HRM has offices all over the world, and I could request another transfer, but how would it look right now? Not great. I haven't been at headquarters long enough to prove myself.

There's only one course of action right now. I need to finish my shower, dry my hair, and gird my loins for the gut-wrenching meeting at ten.

~

My hands tremble over my keyboard all through the morning.

At ten minutes to ten, I lean back in my chair and clench them into fists, stilling my body through sheer force of will.

You are in control of this meeting, I remind myself. *This is your job, and you're great at it.*

My face slips into the neutral expression that I've always worn before high-pressure meetings. A former boss of mine once said that he wondered if anything ever shook me, and I laughed it off. "No," I said. "Nothing ever does." That's the kind of illusion you need to maintain if you're going to work in PR, and I've been damn good at it so far.

Christian has taken me far off that path, but I'm back on it and ready to face him.

That's what I'm telling myself when my phone rings at 9:55.

It's Adam, calling from his desk.

"Campbell," I say, my voice strong and clear. I'll be damned if I let anyone see how much this has shaken me, how much it's made me doubt everything that happened over the past few weeks.

"Mr. Pierce is here for your ten o'clock. Should I send him in?"

"Absolutely," I say, and my heart wrenches in my chest.

Moments later, my office door swings open, Adam holding it, and Christian strides through, his chin up, his back straight. I drop my shoulders a little and lift my chin in answer. Adam gives me a nod and pulls the door closed behind him as Christian crosses the office without a pause and sits down across from me.

He looks like shit.

That's not entirely true. He looks amazing. He always does. He's clean-shaven, giving me an unobstructed view of his chiseled jaw, and his suit is tailored to perfection. I'm sure that what's underneath hasn't changed at all.

But his eyes are filled with pain—and something else.

"Mr. Pierce."

"Ms. Campbell."

His words settle in the air between us. My throat tightens up.

Not now.

I swallow hard and give him a thin-lipped smile. "I'm sorry I had to cancel our meeting last week. I wasn't feeling well." My tone was meant to be confident, but my voice rings false, strained. This isn't what I want to be saying.

"I understand."

"Thank you." I slide a leather portfolio across the desk to him. "This is what I have planned for the upcoming week. If there are any tweaks you'd like me to make in terms of scheduling or venue, I thought we could go over those today."

He reaches out one of his strong hands. I want him to be reaching for me, cupping the side of my face, pressing against the small of my back while he kisses me like tomorrow might never come. Instead he flips open the portfolio and scans the top sheet.

"I have no problem with this schedule."

Christian's voice gives away nothing, but his eyes...

I want to say, *why did you lie to me*? I want to say, *how could you*? I want to say, *take it back*. I want to howl my heartbreak at him.

I say none of those things.

Instead I say, "Wonderful. I won't take up any more of your time today, Mr. Pierce. I'll see you on Monday for the veteran's benefit event."

And then, even as my heart is tearing in two, I rise from my seat and extend my hand across the desk to him.

He rises to meet me, his eyes never leaving mine, and puts out his hand.

Takes mine in his.

Shakes.

Like we're business associates, and nothing more. Yet at the touch of our skin, there it is—that connection, that undeniable recognition...

My heart is never going to be whole again.

He drops my hand and turns to go, and I sit back down, my fists balled in my lap.

Christian pauses, his hand on the door handle, and looks back at me.

"This?" he says, waving his hand between us. "It isn't over."

Then he's gone.

44

CHRISTIAN

I don't know what came over me back there.

That's a lie.

I know exactly what came over me, and what came over me is that I'm in love with Quinn Campbell. I'm in love with her, and there's nothing that anyone can do about it.

On Monday, I put some things into motion. I made a few calls. I consulted with a few people, anonymously, because I'm not as stupid as my decisions make me seem.

With every moment that's passed since I left my father's office on Monday, the way ahead has become clearer and clearer. It's like a light has gone on in my head, illuminating everything I need to do with such clarity that it's blinding.

I don't care.

Getting her back is all that matters.

When I sat down across from Quinn, I saw the struggle in her eyes. I saw what she was trying so valiantly to hide. I saw it in the way there were tiny crescents on two of her knuckles from clenching her hands into fists. I heard it in the tired strain in her voice. And I felt it between us, the connection stretched so tight it's ready to snap.

But it hasn't yet.

That's what buoys me as I get the hell out of HRM's headquarters and slide into the back of the town car.

It's not over for her.

She might tell herself that it is. She might even tell other people—Carolyn comes to mind—that she's done with me. I'm only surprised that Quinn didn't admit it to me during the meeting. She prides herself on honesty. I haven't forgotten how she told me she learned about Elijah—the person she thought was Elijah—while sitting at that very desk. It's not like her to hide things, which means that I hurt her deeply.

It also means that she hasn't made up her mind yet.

She's hedging her bets, not wanting to give up more information than necessary.

Once again, I'm impressed by her professionalism in the face of total devastation.

When I got up to leave, I couldn't keep myself under control any longer. I had to say something, anything, to acknowledge the situation we're in. I certainly didn't plan it, otherwise I'd have said something other than "this isn't over."

Of course it isn't over. If nothing else, we're working with each other until...

Until what? Until she rats me out? She's not going to do that. If she was going to, she'd have done it by now.

What else is there to do?

She could quit.

No, she couldn't. Quinn isn't a quitter. She came out here to build a new life for herself, and she's not the kind of woman who's going to flee the city without giving notice because a new relationship didn't make the cut.

Or so she thinks.

While Louis navigates the town car through the midmorning traffic, I fight the urge to tell him to turn around right now.

It's *not* over.

I want to go back there and explain what I'm planning to do, but it's taking longer than I expected to get all the pieces in place.

There's also the fact that she probably thinks I'm a disturbed liar—a felonious criminal. Maybe she even thinks that I murdered my brother.

It's also entirely possible that I'll be prosecuted for identity theft once...

I can't think about that now.

The only thing that matters to me is how I feel when I'm with Quinn, and how she feels when she's with me. The only thing that matters is *us*.

I close my eyes and think back to the first time I saw her, frantically yanking on the handle of that suitcase, stuck out in the middle of the intersection, the rain cascading down on top of her. I didn't know the first thing about her, but her strength drew me in even then. She hadn't broken down when the jerk in the SUV sent her suitcase flying, didn't crumple onto the sidewalk and cry. She commented on it wryly and then went right back out into the street to collect her sopping wet clothes from the pavement without ever missing a beat.

She's still that woman.

She's still the same woman who decided to give her life in Colorado the middle finger and do something else because, damn it, she wasn't going to live with the memory of her asshole ex-fiancé flung in her face all the time.

So, maybe I'm wrong. Maybe she will leave the city.

But if I know Quinn—and I think I do—she won't leave before I can set things straight.

And I have to make this right with her. Between us.

Louis pulls the town car up to the curb outside the Pierce Industries building, and I step out into the sweltering summer heat. It's miserable in the city right now. I can't wait for autumn.

By the time the leaves fall from the trees, this nightmare will be over, one way or another. I have no idea right now if solving one problem will lead to a thousand more, but now that I've seen Quinn, my mind is made up.

The lobby of the building is blessedly frigid, and I move at a leisurely pace across the lobby to the bank of elevators. Our floor is, obviously, air conditioned as well, but the lobby might as well be a walk-in refrigerator. The cool is amazing on my flushed skin. It's not only the weather that has me hot and bothered, and my heart rate is so high right now that I'm probably in danger of cardiac arrest.

It's time to get this show on the road.

The elevator doors slide open, and I step into the empty car. There are a few things I need to finish up this morning, and at some point—

A man sticks his arm between the closing doors. They stop closing, and then start sliding open again.

It's my new lawyer.

"Mr. Pierce," he says, a sheepish smile on his face. "I was in a bit of a hurry, hoping to meet with you by lunch—"

"Not a problem," I say, smiling back. "We can get started on our business right away."

45

QUINN

The moment Christian is out of my office, I grab for my phone, tugging open the bottom drawer of my desk with so much force that I nearly dump the entire contents of my purse onto the floor in my hurry.

Hands shaking, I type out a message to Carolyn.

She doesn't know everything—she *can't* know everything—but I can't keep this all to myself.

Christian came in for a meeting

I'm fairly certain that she's working at the boutique right now. She's almost always at work. I lay my phone down on the desk and take a deep breath, preparing myself for the agonizing wait.

Her reply comes so quickly it's like she had been holding her phone in her hand, so quickly that the vibration against the glass surface of my desk startles me.

Calm the hell down, Quinn. People are going to think you're having a fit.

What people, I don't know, since I'm alone in the office and Adam calls ahead when there are visitors, but I take another calming breath in through my nose and let it out slowly through my mouth.

OMG. How did it go?

It was weird. And then at the end he said

My thumb slips onto the send button before I can complete the sentence, and while I'm typing out the rest of what I wanted to tell her, Carolyn's reply comes in.

DON'T YOU DARE LEAVE ME HANGING LIKE THAT

Accidental send! He said "This? It isn't over."

What does that mean???

I have no idea.

Wait...was it mutual?

Not really.

What do you mean, not really?

I left him.

Have you talked *about it?*

No.

Carolyn sends an animated emoji of a yellow smiley face rolling its eyes.

I know...

Talk to him, Quinn.

I don't know how to have this conversation.

Yes you do.

It won't fix anything.

How do you know?

I know, okay?

Then why are you texting me about what he said?

I pause.

I have to know.

If I don't find out why Christian did what he did, I'll spend the rest of my life wondering, and I can't do that. Could it honestly be that he couldn't bear to face his father, knowing that his favorite son was dead?

The blood drains from my face. Christian lied to me. There's no way around that. But he could have been telling me the truth last Thursday, too.

I had every right to be upset about him lying to me. I still have every right to be upset.

But Christian is human, like the rest of us. And from what I can tell, he didn't get anything extra out of pretending to be his brother, other than his father's affection.

I never doubted that my father loved me. Not everyone in the world has it so easy.

Even billionaires have their problems.

Nope. *No.*

I need to shut this down. I can't keep spending time justifying his actions. I'm not ready to forgive him and move on from this. I'm in New York City because another man lied to me so well and for so long that by the time I left, he had another life waiting for him in the wings. With my *best friend.*

It's not my job to let Christian off the hook. My biggest responsibility is to live a life that I want to live, and right now—as gut-wrenching as it is to admit it—that life does not include a lying billionaire who is still, to this day, impersonating his dead twin brother.

And yet...

And *yet*...

I send another message to Carolyn.

I want some closure.

Are you sure that's all you want?

Yes.

Then I'm with you 100%.

The bubble indicating that she's typing again pops up right away.

I agree, though—what a bizarre thing to say!

I drop my phone back into my purse and flick on my computer screen, an odd wave of focus coming over me.

I can take charge of my own life.

It won't be the first time I've done it, and it won't be the last, but I need to do something right now to make a change. It will put my mind at ease. It will put a stop to this endless second-guessing about a relationship that probably wasn't going to go anywhere.

Sooner or later, the truth was going to come out. There isn't a person on earth who could keep a secret like that for a lifetime. Jesus, what if we'd been married? What if I'd been *pregnant*?

I need to put myself back in the driver's seat, and I know how I'm going to do it.

I stand up from my desk and glance at my reflection in the office window, tugging my blazer so that it lays smoothly over my curves. Then I'm in motion, out the door.

"Adam, call Walker and tell him I'm coming down for a meeting."

"Of course, Ms. Campbell," Adam calls out to my retreating back.

Walker's office is on the opposite end of the floor, so it takes me a little longer than I'd like to get there. Quite a few people greet me as I go past, and I stop to chat with most of them. I've always made it a habit to be a charmer in the office. You never know when those connections might come in handy.

Finally, Walker's secretary—who is constantly on the phone —waves me in with a smile.

"Thanks, Marjorie," I mouth, and go in through Walker's open door.

He turns away from his computer when he hears me enter. "Quinn," he says with a broad grin. "Adam said you were on your way. What can I do for you?"

I sit down in one of the two chairs across from Walker's desk and cross my legs, making sure my posture is straight and confident. "You know how much I love it here at HRM, don't you?"

A flicker of confusion crosses his face, but his smile doesn't waver. "You're doing quite the job with the Pierce account," Walker laughs. "If you hated it here, there's no way you'd put in that kind of effort."

"The thing is—working on the Pierce account has opened my eyes. I don't want to leave HRM. I want to go...*bigger*." I raise my hands in front of me, giving Walker an approximation of the size of my dreams. I let my smile extend all the way to my eyes.

He cocks his head and considers me. "What do you mean by bigger? Are you requesting a transfer? There's only one office that..." His mouth drops open. "You're an ambitious one. Are you talking about what I think you're talking about?"

"Yes," I say, my voice strong and enthusiastic. "*London*."

46

CHRISTIAN

This is what my life has come to.

I'm standing in the Pierce Industries lobby on Friday morning with a black portfolio in my hand. Frank, my lawyer, stands at my side.

"This isn't a requirement," he says for the hundredth time. "We can begin private negotiations on this issue without letting the world know through a press conference. The news will break eventually. It doesn't have to happen today. As your lawyer, it's my duty to advise you that this—"

"I know," I say quickly, cutting him off. "I know, Frank, but this is what I have to do. The thing starts in five minutes. Are you going to stand here trying to talk me out of it until the last second?"

He shakes his head, then pats my shoulder. "I had to try one more time."

"Glad it was the last one."

The press is gathering on the sidewalk. Two different

networks have cameras here, and there are reporters from three print outlets, plus the usual cadre of bloggers who show up whenever someone from a multinational corporation holds a press conference.

Good, I think. She can't miss this.

In fact, I'm going to make sure she doesn't miss this.

She can't miss this, because from what I understand, this is my last chance.

The text from Carolyn came in late Wednesday night.

You up?

Always :)

Ha.

What do you need?

Chris, I don't know what's going on between you and Q. None of my business. Don't need to know the details on your end unless you want to tell me. But she told me this evening that she started talking to HRM about a transfer to London. If everything works out, she'll be gone in a matter of weeks.

Thanks for letting me know, my friend.

Welcome.

I haven't talked to Carolyn in person since she got busy with her boutique and I stopped frequenting the Swan quite as much, so I don't know how pissed she is at me for fooling around with her roommate's heart. Obviously she's not too pissed, otherwise she wouldn't have given me a heads up, but it's probably time to have a conversation with her once this news breaks.

I called my lawyer within five minutes of receiving her message and told him to move everything up to the earliest possible date. If I'm going to do this, it has to be now.

Three minutes to go. This news is going to do more than break.

It's going to explode.

Two minutes. I pull my phone out of my pocket and swipe to unlock the screen. Quinn's office number is the first contact on my list.

Adam takes the call.

"Quinn Campbell's office."

"This is Christian Pierce. Is Ms. Campbell available to speak with me?"

"Her line is clear. Hold one moment, please."

"Thank you."

There's a muted silence as Adam transfers the call, and then a click as Quinn picks up her handset.

"Quinn Campbell."

Her voices makes my heart skip a beat. Am I imagining the hitch I heard in the breath she took right after she answered?

"Pull up a window on your computer and start streaming ABC7." Their camera guy is fifteen feet away from me right now, fiddling with the tech at his shoulder. The anchor is a tall redhead in a coral jacket standing to the right of his elbow. In another minute, they'll be broadcasting my announcement to the entire city. Perhaps the entire world.

The anchor looks down and presses a finger to her ear—listening to whatever's coming in from the studio, probably.

"What?" Quinn asks, her voice pure worry. "Why? Did something happen?"

It hits me all at once that Quinn might be imagining some kind of terrorist situation.

"I'm holding a press conference outside the offices of Pierce Industries."

"*What*?" I hear papers rustling in the background, a series of clicks. "We didn't plan for—what are you *doing*?"

"I'm telling the truth."

Before she can say another word, I disconnect the call, then flip through my settings, shutting down every possible ring-tone and chime. I hand the phone to my lawyer, who tucks it into his leather portfolio. He'll hold it for me while I'm making my remarks so there's no chance of me doing something idiotic like dropping it on the sidewalk. He was a stickler on that point. Why, I don't know.

I've been relatively calm, but now that the press is beginning to focus all their attention on the podium, my heart beats faster.

This is it.

This is the moment I thought would never come, and now I'm the one forcing it to happen.

Frank puts his hand on my shoulder in a show of strength and support, turns me toward him, and then looks me up and down. I follow his gaze, making sure that my jacket is buttoned, my fly is zipped, there are no errant threads, no pieces of lint—nothing to distract from my message. Quinn herself has done the same thing many times since we started working together.

I wish she was doing it right now. I wish it was her by my side. Frank's a good guy, but nobody holds a candle to Quinn.

I steel myself. This is the only way I'll ever have a chance at getting her back. If I want her to stand by my side at any point in the future, moving past this is the only option.

"You ready?" Frank asks, looking directly into my eyes. This is my final chance to back out. I know he'd happily go out and tell the press that there had been a mistake, that there would be no announcement today.

"Let's get this shit over with."

He gives me a confident nod, and then we both head toward the front doors.

The sun is hot, beating down on the shoulders of my suit. I'm trapped in a furnace—that's how it feels.

As we discussed in advance, Frank approaches the podium first. "Christian Pierce of Pierce Industries," he says simply. The reporters shift their weight from foot to foot. One blogger raises his hand as if he wants to ask Frank a question before this circus has even started, but then decides better of it.

I move to the podium and open the portfolio, sliding the sheet of paper with my remarks—written in a large font in case I lose my ability to see clearly—out of the protective pocket.

I clear my throat, scan the words on the page, then look directly into the ABC7 camera. Conveniently, they've positioned themselves right in front of the podium.

I swallow hard.

Everyone holds their breath.

Somewhere across the city, Quinn is watching.

"Good morning," I begin, my voice confident and clear. "My name is Elijah Pierce. Ten years ago, my brother, Christian Pierce, died of a drug overdose at a party being held to celebrate our eighteenth birthday. At that time, distraught and traumatized, I assumed his identity. I have been using his name and living as Christian Pierce since that time."

They don't wait until I read the rest of my statement to start shouting questions.

47

QUINN

I'm frozen in place behind my desk, hand covering my mouth.

It's like he's talking to *me.* Right through the screen. Admitting everything.

"Good morning," he says, his voice steady, without an ounce of shame. "My name is Elijah Pierce. Ten years ago, my brother, Christian Pierce, died of a drug overdose at a party being held to celebrate our eighteenth birthday. At that time, distraught and traumatized, I assumed his identity. I have been using his name and living as Christian Pierce since that time."

Holy *shit.*

The press surrounding him—I can't see how many people there are because obviously ABC isn't going to put competitors on camera—pounces the instant Christian stops speaking to take a breath. He tries unsuccessfully to quiet them, and finally his lawyer steps up to the podium, waving them down.

"One question at a time, please," he calls, once, twice, three times, and finally there's a semblance of silence.

A woman's arm, covered by the sleeve of a coral jacket, juts into the frame, holding out a microphone. "Mr. Pierce, why are you revealing this information on broadcast news? Has your family been informed?"

Again, Christian looks right into the camera.

"I wanted the world to know the truth," he says, and my heart bursts.

"Why did you do it?" pipes up a male voice from somewhere off-camera.

"It was my impression that my father had a closer connection with my brother," Christian says, not hesitating for a single moment. "In my devastation, I made a snap decision to spare my father the pain of losing his favorite son."

In another instant, I'm up out of my seat, grabbing for my purse. This time it does tip, spilling half of what's inside into my desk drawer. The only thing I stop to grab is my wallet, and I shove my phone inside on my way out the door.

I don't care what they think. I'm going.

"I'm going out," I shout to Adam on my way past his desk, and he does a double take when he sees me moving at such a high speed on three-inch heels. "If Walker asks, you can tell him it was a client emergency."

That's what this is, after all. My one and only client has taken it upon himself to schedule and follow through on a press conference during which he has announced information fit to destroy his reputation completely. There's a good chance I might get fired for this—I've seen people let go from HRM for less. All I can do now is rush to the scene of the disaster and try to spin it.

Of course, even as I sprint for the elevator, I know that's not why I'm fleeing the building.

I'm running to Christian's side because he did this—all of this—for *me*.

He didn't have to tell the world his secret or hold a press conference and announce it to countless people who happen to be watching the news. He ensured that the story will be picked up by every gossip blog and every news outlet from here to Los Angeles. This is going to be big news, and he refused to use the services of the person hired to manage his reputation.

He didn't let anything soften the blow.

For all I know, the punches are still coming.

I have to get to him.

I run through the building's lobby and slam my hands against the door, almost losing my balance as I throw myself out onto the sidewalk.

Cab. I need a cab.

I look left, then look right as the heat descends like a heavy blanket over the back of my neck.

Every cab for as far as I can see is occupied, and not a single one of them is pulling up to the curb to let someone out.

Pierce Industries is four blocks away.

I've never been there because we've always scheduled the PR meetings at HRM, I *always* know the fastest way to my clients at all times.

I give myself five more seconds to hail a cab, and when none appear, I take off running down the sidewalk, thanking my lucky stars that I've always been a natural in heels.

I'm instantly sweltering in the morning sun, and after a block I'm hugging the inside of the street, praying for awnings, but I don't slow down. I move, move, move until I'm forced to stop by a do not walk sign—God help you if you cross against the light in New York City, and even if you're walking with it, *things can happen*—taking off again as soon as the white hand blinks on.

The second block goes by in a blur of restaurants and people, some of whom actually step out of the way of the crazed woman running down the sidewalk at top speed in high heels, clutching her purse like she's pursuing a thief.

Two blocks left, and the heat is getting to me.

I have to get there.

I have to tell him, right now, that I saw what he did, and that it means everything to me. I know he's telling the truth. I know he's fully aware that looking into the camera will bring people swooping in to investigate his every claim, and if they are not truthful, he will be eviscerated in the press and quite possibly arrested and sent to prison for identity theft.

One more block.

As I sprint across the intersection, blisters rising on my heels and the bottom of my feet, a couple of businessmen turn and step out of my way. It's then that I see him, halfway down the block.

I slow to a half jog, not wanting to barrel into a crowd of reporters looking like a desperate, hot mess.

His lawyer steps up to the podium and raises both hands, saying something I can't hear, and then both men turn their backs to the press gaggle and start to walk back toward the entrance. A heavily muscled man in a dark suit comes out of the building and stands in front of the doors, crossing his arms over his chest. Security to keep the press out.

I pick up the pace, hurrying toward them. This is going to be a complete pain in the ass if I don't get there before he goes inside, an awkward phone call so that the guard knows to let me in, another fifteen minutes in the heat in front of the cameras, who will linger long enough to get more b-roll and film the reporter segments...

Suddenly, I'm overwhelmed by the need to get to Christian —Elijah?—I can't keep it straight—*right now*. As soon as he steps back into the building, he's going to be surrounded by people demanding to know everything, and once that happens, all bets are off. I might not be able to get to him even if I can get inside.

Christian turns and looks back over his shoulder. Over the traffic noise, I can't tell if he's responding to another question or telling them that the interview is over, but it buys me another few seconds...

His lawyer reaches out, puts a hand on his shoulder, and

both men turn back toward the doors. I hustle forward, but my shoes cut into my feet, a searing line of pain where the skin has rubbed raw. I can't—

"Christian!" I shout.

He doesn't hear me, but a couple of the bloggers look my way. I don't give a shit.

"*Christian*!" I shout again, at the top of my lungs, and now they're all looking at me.

Christian's lawyer nudges his arms, and he turns.

I can't stop myself. It hurts like a bitch, running with the skin on my feet in this condition, but I don't care, I go toward him like there's no time left.

For all I know, maybe there isn't.

His face is a mask of confusion, but as I come closer his eyes widen with surprise, and then, as he registers the expression on my face, delight.

I barrel into him, still moving so quickly that it almost takes both of us to the ground.

And then, in a completely unprofessional display, I lock my arms around his neck and kiss him like I've never kissed anyone before in my life, like we're alone in his bedroom, like this kiss will be enough to heal all the wounds between us, like I never want to stop.

I am lost in him. I never care to be found.

We kiss for so long that when we come up for air, I'm gasping for breath. Christian's arms lock around me, our cheeks pressed together.

"I did it for you," he says, his voice heavy and thick.

There's nothing I can think of to say, except:

"I know. I love you. I *love* you."

48

CHRISTIAN

Everything is complete chaos from the very moment I end the press conference, but there's nothing comparable to when Quinn comes sprinting down the sidewalk in the summer heat and our bodies connect with such force that despite my strength, we almost end up sprawled out on the sidewalk on national television.

Not that it would matter much. Now that I've revealed a secret that's sure to shock the nation, falling down probably wouldn't get much press coverage.

Although, with the Internet, you never know.

Her kiss is powerful, furious, full of forgiveness.

It takes me by surprise, and at the same time, it's exactly what I would expect out of a love like ours.

I want to tell her that her presence is a balm on my aching heart, that I would have done all this for her and more, that I know there's a long road ahead of us, that I know this is the start.

Instead, I choke out the only words I can muster: "I did it for you."

And Quinn says the only words I want to hear. "I know. I love you. I *love* you."

It's only when I'm finally able to loosen my grip on her, to pull myself away, that we both become aware, once again, of the cameras, of the bloggers with their phones out, filming every moment of our reunion, and of the kiss, and inevitable live broadcasting of it to their audiences.

All across the country, I'm absolutely positive that we're making headlines.

I don't care.

All I care about is that she came back to me, and we have another chance.

I wipe the grin off my face and give the press a serious expression, then nod my head, steer Quinn by the elbow, and guide her inside the lobby, Frank on our heels.

Once we're in the cool of the lobby, he bursts out laughing. "Boy, what a display!" he says, shaking his head. "I'll give you two a moment. That was incredible. My God."

He walks away, hands in his pockets, probably wondering how he lucked into a client like me.

Quinn is still catching her breath, but she instantly reaches for my hand and squeezes it. Her eyes are a mixture of confusion and relief and love and every other possible emotion under the sun.

She opens her mouth to speak, then closes it again. Her green eyes narrow.

"I don't know what to call you, now that—" She gives a little shrug.

I do. I know.

"My name is Elijah Pierce," I say, releasing her hand, stepping back, and extending my right hand as if we're meeting for the first time. "It's an absolute pleasure to meet you."

Quinn takes my hand with a smile and shakes with the same firm confidence as the first time we shook hands, six weeks and a million years ago in her office. "Quinn Campbell," she answers. "Your girlfriend. If you'll have me."

I pull her into my arms and hug her again, kissing the smooth skin of her cheek, slightly dewy from sprinting up to the building. "I think the better question is, will you have me? I know I'm not the man you thought you knew."

"Aren't you?" she says, pulling back and searching my eyes, her gaze intense. "I'm not sure that's true, Chr—Elijah," she says, correcting herself at the last moment. "Maybe you played a part sometimes, like when I saw you at the Swan, but I've seen the real you, too. Very real, if you know what I mean." Quinn's eyes are sparkling, and I get flashes of all the time we've spent in bed together. My cock hardens, pressing against my zipper. "You know," she continues, her voice thoughtful. "There could be a part of you—the real you—who likes to be the center of attention. It doesn't have to be all or nothing."

Quinn's words hit me like a sucker punch delivered by a choir of angels.

It doesn't have to be all or nothing.

It's true.

I can enjoy the company of my friends and close down the Swan *and* be the kind of guy who wants to settle down with a woman, keeping her close to me for the rest of my life.

Whether my friends will still want to see me is a question that remains to be answered.

I scoop her up into my arms and kiss her on the cheek again, then take her by the shoulders and look deeply into those glinting green eyes. "You're a wonder, Quinn."

She grins up at me. After a moment, though, her face turns serious.

"Eli—can I call you Eli?"

"You can call me whatever you want."

"Have you talked to your father yet?"

~

The ride up to my father's floor seems endless, but Quinn holds my hand tightly in hers all the way up, standing by my side in comfortable silence.

My heart pounds.

My father will have heard the news by now, if he didn't see it being broadcast live. He and his staff don't miss much.

I'm not surprised when his secretary stares up at me from her seat, then inclines her head toward the door.

I take both Quinn's hands in mine outside the entrance to his office and kiss her gently.

"I'll wait out here," she says softly, then gives me an encouraging smile.

As I go into my father's office, I hear his secretary already remembering her manners. "Can I get you anything to drink?"

Quinn's reply is cut off as I close the door behind me.

It takes an enormous effort to look up from my shoes and into my father's eyes.

When I do, I get the shock of a lifetime.

He doesn't look angry.

In fact, he's smiling at me, with tears in his eyes.

"Dad?" I say, my voice choked.

He gets up from behind his desk, crosses the space between us, and enfolds me in his arms.

"Eli," he says softly, and I hug him back. "You've returned."

"What?" I say, pulling back so I can look into his eyes. "You knew it was me all along?"

He laughs, stepping back to put a little breathing room between us. "I was there the moment you were born, Elijah. Did you think I would forget which one of my sons was which?"

I am overwhelmed with confusion. "But why did you—"

"Let this little game of yours go on so long?" He shakes his head. "I never expected it to last a decade, for one. There were many times I thought I might—I thought I might say something, give myself away, but every time, I held back."

"*Why*?"

He puts a hand to his mouth and thinks for a moment before he answers. "Losing a child was the worst thing that ever happened to me," he says, his voice low and soft. "I can't imagine what it was like to lose an identical twin. Your grief must have been—it must have been overpowering.

"At first I thought it was something you'd snap out of, but as the months went by and became years, it seemed like something you needed to do."

My mouth drops open. The lengths my father has gone to to indulge me in this are beyond what anyone could expect from any father.

"But...you had him buried under my name."

"I did." This might be the first time he's ever admitted it out loud to anyone. "I did do that. Seems pretty fucked up, doesn't it?" My father grins despite the tears in his eyes. "I guess I'm...what, an accomplice?"

"You didn't have to do that." The lump in my throat threatens to turn to tears.

"I did. Because one of my sons was still alive, and for whatever reason, he needed to be his brother."

I turn away, covering my eyes with my hands. "You always... you always liked him better."

"What can I say? I was an asshole when you were growing up. But I didn't like him better. I wanted you to enjoy the things we enjoyed. It was a bad way to go about it."

"Yeah, it was," I agree heartily, and we both laugh. "Jesus Christ. I am in such deep shit."

"No doubt about that, son," my dad says.

Relief. Sweet relief.

"I can't believe you let me get away with that for a *decade*."

My father is silent for a moment, and then he looks me straight in the eye. "As ridiculous as it sounds...it was a way for me to have both of my sons. At least for a while."

I look toward the ceiling and consider the pair of us, each devastated by the loss of my brother, each reacting in what might have been the most idiotic way possible. "Damn, do we need *therapy*."

We laugh at that for a long time.

My gut is aching with laughter, but when it finally subsides, I have one more thing to say to my father.

"Dad, remember when we had that conversation about finding a good woman?"

"Yes?" His brow wrinkles.

"Well, she didn't exactly keep me out of the gossip sites. I screwed that one up."

"I'd say. That press conference is going to be pretty hard to spin."

I wave that comment away. We can talk about all that later, but even so, I'm not worried about Pierce Industries. If anything, the extra coverage will boost its stock price.

"The important thing is..." My voice trails off. I'm relishing this moment so much that I'm already nostalgic for it.

"Spit it out, Eli."

I've never smiled so brightly as in that moment.

"There's someone I'd like you to meet."

EPILOGUE

QUINN

Three months later

The podium is already in place outside of the Pierce Industries building, and Eli—it's still hard for me to think of him as Eli and not Christian, even now—can hardly stand still. He's about to announce that he's been cleared of any wrongdoing by the federal government, which—wouldn't you know it—takes identity theft pretty seriously, and that all the charges against him have been dropped.

"It's good to be a free man," he says, watching the press gather outside.

I roll my eyes. "You've always been a free man. It's not like they made you wait in prison."

"They *could* have made me wait in prison."

"There's no amount of bail that Pierce Industries wouldn't have paid, and we both know it."

Eli shrugs, still grinning at me.

An elevator dings its arrival across the lobby, and I turn to see his father, Harlan Pierce, step out.

That whole story—what a doozy.

The moment they stepped out of his office together three months ago, it was clear that any past misunderstandings had been cleared up—or at least forgiven for the time being.

"Quinn Campbell!" said Harlan Pierce jovially, and I shook his hand with an air of joyful confusion.

"You don't seem very surprised by this news, sir," I couldn't help saying.

He winked at me. "It's hard to surprise a man who's known you your entire life."

"I'll take your word for it."

From then on, Christian and his father were genuinely close. Once a month, they've been attending therapy sessions together. I can't imagine having to do that with my own father, who has thoroughly enjoyed his life in a small town in Northern Michigan. The last time we argued was when I was in high school and going through a rebellious phase.

"Hello, lovebirds," he calls now, striding across the lobby. He can't wait to stand next to his son while he makes this announcement. It's not likely to be the last of the press coverage about the strange story of Elijah and Christian Pierce, but at least it's a relatively happy ending.

"Mr. Pierce," I say, greeting him with a smile.

"Is this one all ready to go?" he asks me, putting an arm around Eli's shoulders.

Eli shrugs him off good-naturedly. "I'm standing right here," he jokes.

"He's as ready as he'll ever be," I say, then take Eli's arm and turn him toward me. I give him a once-over, making sure his outfit is in pristine condition, then straighten his tie.

The press looks to be fully assembled, and it's supposed to rain later this afternoon—they won't stay long if we don't give them something to pay attention to. "Let's go entertain our guests."

"As you wish," Eli says, raising my hand to his lips and kissing it theatrically.

"My goodness," I say, teasing. "Keep yourself under control. We are at *work*."

Not long after that insanely hot kiss on camera brought down the wrath of HRM's management upon my head, I got to build a press release announcing my new position at Pierce Industries as Vice President of Reputation Management. I forced Harlan to put me through the full interview process, even though he created the position for me.

I'm not harboring any guilt about that. I'm good at my job. I can't help that I'm in love with the boss's son, and that Pierce Industries can use a top-of-the-line public relations professional on their staff.

I lead the way out onto the sidewalk. The fall air is pleasant—not too hot, not too cold—and the cloud cover is easy on the eyes.

I step up to the podium with confidence and wait for the chatter among the reporters to stop.

"Thanks for being here, everybody," I say, scanning the crowd. "Harlan and Elijah Pierce of Pierce Industries."

Then I step back, ceding the podium.

The two men step up in front of it together, Harlan slightly to one side, and Eli takes a folded piece of paper from his pocket and smooths it against the polished mahogany surface of the podium. "Hello, everyone," he says with a half smile that has me wet in an instant.

A shiver of pleasure goes through me when I think of what we're going to do in bed later...

Snap out of it, Quinn. You're on camera!

Eli is halfway through his statement. "—pleased to announce that I have been cleared of all wrongdoing. I thank you all for your support during this difficult time, and I look forward to sharing the future success of Pierce Industries with you."

Unsurprisingly, there are no questions. Almost to a one, everyone gathered in front of the podium waits to see if Eli is going to announce anything groundbreaking. This is not *nearly* as exciting as his last press conference.

Harlan and Eli exchange a look, and then Harlan steps off to the side.

I'm instantly on edge. This isn't the plan. Harlan was supposed to make a short statement in support of his son, and then take a few questions. What is he doing?

Eli pulls another piece of paper from his breast pocket,

unfolds it, scans it for a moment, and tucks it into the podium. Then he turns and gestures for me to come forward.

I arrive at the podium as he steps to the opposite side, in plain view of the reporters.

"Eli—what—"

"Quinn Campbell," he says, his voice clear as a bell. The three anchors who have assembled each thrust their microphones another inch closer to us, desperate to pick up every word. "There's so much I want to say to you that I can't possibly fit it all in during this press conference."

What is he *doing*?

"I loved you almost from the moment I saw you," he continues, and it dawns on me.

This is a proposal.

Oh, my *god*.

My heart soars.

"I never want to spend another day without you by my side." Eli gets down on one knee and pulls a small velvet box from his pocket and opening it to reveal a diamond set in a ring of sapphires. It's the most beautiful piece of jewelry I've ever seen, and perfectly unconventional. "Will you give me the chance to spend the rest of my life telling you, every day, how much I love you?"

A happy tear spills out of the corner of my eye, and with a trembling hand I wipe it away.

"There's nothing else I'd rather do," I choke out.

"Is that a yes?" says Eli, a cheeky smile on his face.

"Yes!" I cry, and then throw myself into his arms. Laughing, he stands up, lifting us both, and kisses me long and hard, right on the mouth, for all the world to see.

For more books by Amelia Wilde, visit her online at
www.awilderomance.com

CPSIA information can be obtained
at www.ICGtesting.com
Printed in the USA
LVOW10s1756091117
555649LV00012B/565/P